Josh inserted the
Suddenly the door b
open. Something wha
chair, and an arm snak

'Eyyoww!' Josh yelled as he was sent flying.
'What kind of a raving maniac— Rob!'

Josh gaped as Rob hastily ejected the disk from
the machine. 'What are you playing at?'

'Just in the nick of time!' Rob replied. He
looked at Josh, who was busy untangling himself
from his upended chair. 'Don't you know what
an arachnid is, Josh? It's a spider!'

Josh was about to say something when the full
meaning of Rob's words hit him. He sat there on
the floor with his mouth hanging open.

'A spider? Then I nearly walked into a Black
Widow trap!'

INTERNET DETECTIVES

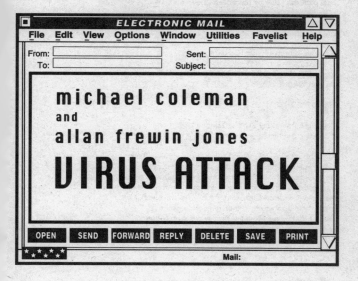

ELECTRONIC MAIL

File Edit View Options Window Utilities Favelist Help

From: Sent:
To: Subject:

michael coleman
and
allan frewin jones
VIRUS ATTACK

OPEN   SEND   FORWARD   REPLY   DELETE   SAVE   PRINT

Mail:

A WORKING PARTNERS BOOK

MACMILLAN CHILDREN'S BOOKS

First published 1997 by Macmillan Children's Books
a division of Macmillan Publishers Limited
25 Eccleston Place, London SW1W 9NF
and Basingstoke

Associated companies throughout the world

Created by Working Partners Limited
London W6 0HE

ISBN 0 330 35112 5

9 8 7 6 5 4 3 2 1

A CIP catalogue record for this book is available from
the British Library.

Printed and bound in Great Britain by Mackays of Chatham plc, Kent

Abbey School, Portsmouth, England.
Monday 14th October, 11.58 a.m.

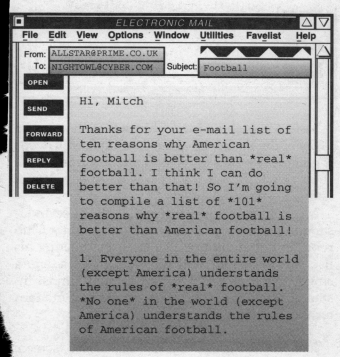

ELECTRONIC MAIL △ ▽

File   Edit   View   Options   Window   Utilities   Favelist   Help

From: ALLSTAR@PRIME.CO.UK
To: NIGHTOWL@CYBER.COM   Subject: Football

OPEN

SEND

FORWARD

REPLY

DELETE

Hi, Mitch

Thanks for your e-mail list of ten reasons why American football is better than *real* football. I think I can do better than that! So I'm going to compile a list of *101* reasons why *real* football is better than American football!

1. Everyone in the entire world (except America) understands the rules of *real* football. *No one* in the world (except America) understands the rules of American football.

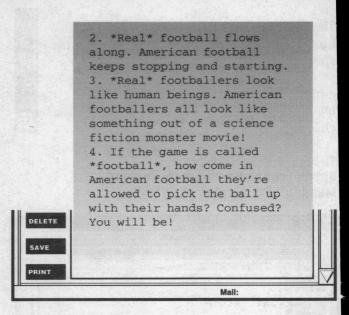

```
2. *Real* football flows
along. American football
keeps stopping and starting.
3. *Real* footballers look
like human beings. American
footballers all look like
something out of a science
fiction monster movie!
4. If the game is called
*football*, how come in
American football they're
allowed to pick the ball up
with their hands? Confused?
You will be!
```

DELETE

SAVE

PRINT

Mail:

Josh Allan chuckled to himself as he tapped away at the keyboard of the computer. Mitch was a good pal – one of several friends from other countries Josh and his friends at Abbey School had made over the Internet.

Mitch Zanelli lived in New York, three thousand miles away from the school Computer Club room in Portsmouth where Josh was making his list. But once Josh had finished his message, a single touch of a key would send it almost instantaneously to Mitch. The wonders of modern technology!

'What's so funny?'

Josh looked over the top of his PC screen.

Tamsyn Smith's eyes were frowning at him over her computer, her inquisitive face framed by short dark hair.

'Mitch,' answered Josh. 'I'm replying to that e-mail he sent about American football. Never let it be said that Josh Allan failed to rise to a challenge.'

He explained his intention of coming up with 101 answers for Mitch.

'Yes, well, I'm sure that's very interesting and worthwhile,' Tamsyn said drily. 'But could you do it without all the chortling, please? I'm trying to read!'

Tamsyn had downloaded the complete text of Charles Dickens' short story *A Christmas Carol* onto her computer from the Net. She had just got to the part where Marley's ghost had appeared, dragging chains along behind him and generally scaring old Ebenezer Scrooge witless. It was a little difficult to maintain the spookiness of the story with Josh chuckling away to himself across the desk.

'I'll be as quiet as a mouse,' Josh said, picking up his computer mouse and waving it at Tamsyn. 'Squeak! Squeak!'

With a sigh, Tamsyn shook her head and went back to her reading. Charles Dickens was her favourite author at the moment. She was working her way steadily through his entire output.

She could hear Josh tapping away and occasionally giggling to himself. It was lucky for him that he was such a good friend, or she'd—

'What on earth!' Tamsyn yelled as she stared in utter disbelief at the PC screen. 'Josh!'

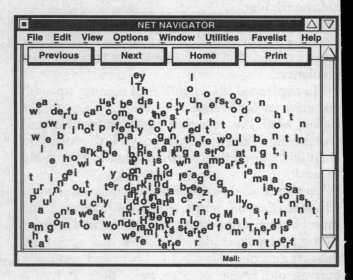

Josh looked up from his keyboard as she yelled. He couldn't believe his eyes. His shock of uncombed dark hair almost stood on end. His e-mail to Mitch was tumbling away down the screen like confetti at a wedding.

'What? I didn't do anything!' Josh howled. The snowfall of letters ended, leaving only a few letters on the otherwise blank screen.

In front of her screen Tamsyn cautiously tapped a key. Nothing happened. The computer seemed to have just died right in front of her eyes. It couldn't be a power failure, because the screen was still live, and she could hear the soft hum of the fan in the back of the machine.

'Maybe this has happened to someone else's computer too?' Josh said. The Abbey school computers had recently been networked, which meant that every computer in the entire school was linked together.

The purpose behind this was so that all the computers could communicate quickly and easily with one another and share software and information.

And Abbey certainly did have plenty of computers. The Computer Club room alone contained four, and there were another dozen or so in the Technology Block, not to mention the several others used for school work in other classrooms. It was the pride of the Abbey School that they had more computers per pupil than any other school in the area.

Josh tried to exit his e-mail application, but the computer screen remained static. He tapped the escape key several times.

Rapid footsteps echoed along the corridor and the door to the Club room came bursting open. It was Mr Findlay, head of the Design and Technology Department. He looked distraught.

'Has anyone just put a new disk in?' he shouted. 'Josh? Are you playing a new game?'

'No, sir,' Josh said. 'I was just—'

'Did you go into any of the system files?' asked Mr Findlay, approaching Josh's computer.

'No.'

Mr Findlay leaned over Josh's shoulder while the others looked on. He tapped a few keys.

'There are no system messages indicating failure,' he said.

Tamsyn looked at him.

'What does that mean, then?' she asked.

Mr Findlay looked up at her.

'It's a virus!' Mr Findlay exclaimed. 'It *must* be a virus.'

'A virus?' said Josh. 'One of those nasty programs that are made to mess up computers?'

'I'm afraid so,' Mr Findlay said. 'But how did it get into the system? I've told people not to bring games into school. Talk about the perfect way to celebrate my birthday! This was all I needed!'

He gave the static computer screen a despairing glance.

'I'd best check some of the other computers. Don't do anything until I come back.' He ran out and they heard him yelling in another classroom in the block.

'OK, Josh, what did you do?' Tamsyn and Josh turned at the sound of Rob's voice from the door.

'Not guilty. Not this time!' Josh said, holding his hands up in mock surrender. 'I didn't do nuffin', honest.'

Rob Zanelli smiled. 'A likely story.' He wheeled himself into the room. Rob had been confined to a wheelchair for the past five years, ever since he had been seriously injured in a road accident at the age of eight. He shared his last name with their American Net friend

Mitch, but so far as they knew, they weren't related.

'Mr Findlay's having kittens!' Rob said. 'I've just passed him now. Apparently every computer in the school has gone down. They're jammed solid.'

A look of astonishment crossed his face as he stared at Tamsyn's screen.

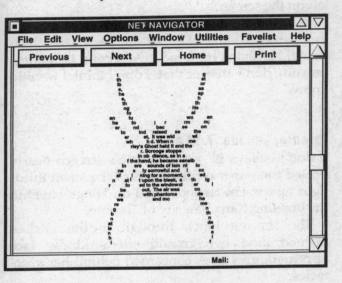

'Tamsyn?' he breathed. 'What kind of program were you running?'

'Huh? What are you talking about?' Tamsyn glanced back at her screen. 'I was just reading *A Christmassss*— Ohhh!'

'It's a spider!' Rob said.

'A what?' Josh dived around to Tamsyn's side

of the desk. He took one look and then ran back to his own screen. His typing hadn't been so dense, so the outline wasn't as clear as on Tamsyn's screen – but the spider shape was there as well.

He looked over the top of the PC at Tamsyn's shocked face and then past her to where Rob sat as if transfixed by the creepy shape that had been left on the screen.

'What kind of a weirdo would plant a virus that leaves a thing like that on the screen?' Josh asked. He shook his head. 'On second thoughts,' he said, 'don't answer that. I don't think I want to know!'

Toronto, Canada. 7.30 a.m.

'I don't believe it!' Lauren King's screech nearly peeled the paper off the walls of the small third-floor apartment she occupied on Yonge Street in the bustling Canadian city of Toronto.

The serving hatch through to the kitchen opened, and her grandmother's kindly face appeared, grey eyes concerned behind her spectacles.

'What in heaven's name has happened?' her grandmother asked.

'I hate Lester Pig!' Lauren exploded. 'I hate Lester Pig to little pieces!'

'Then don't you eat it, honey,' her gran chuckled, 'and I won't buy it again!'

Mad as she was, Lauren couldn't help but

laugh. Her gran came into the living room with a plate of waffles drenched in maple syrup. Lauren's favourite breakfast.

'Oh, Allie,' Lauren growled, 'it's really not funny!' She glared at the screen of the computer that nestled in the corner of their lounge. 'Lester Pig is the person I've been playing chess with for the past three weeks.'

Her gran smiled ruefully. 'Lost again, huh?'

'Yes! Again!' Lauren had a chess board set up next to the computer. An e-mail glowed on the screen.

```
Rook to King's pawn three.
Checkmate yet again, I think!
```

Eleven-year-old Lauren had lived with her plump, beloved granny ever since her parents had drowned in a boating tragedy. They both liked to surf the net, and Lauren, who kept her age secret so she could interact equally with older surfers, had a very good opinion of her own intellect. That was why it was so galling to find a contact on the net who consistently beat her at chess the way Lester Pig did.

'It wouldn't be so bad,' Lauren mumbled through a mouthful of waffle, 'if it wasn't for the fact that I deliberately advertised in the Games Site for someone to play with. And it wouldn't be half so annoying,' she continued, jabbing a syrupy finger at the screen, 'if Lester Pig hadn't put in that little "yet again, I think!" I've never met such a smug, sarcastic, irritating person.'

'If it upsets you that much,' her gran said reasonably, 'maybe you should stop playing with him, uh, her. Which is it, honey?'

'Dunno,' Lauren shrugged. 'I never asked. We don't chat much.' She nodded thoughtfully. 'I'm kind of hoping it's a woman, though. I don't mind being beaten by a woman so much. At least it's not Josh!'

Several months ago Lauren and Josh had played a whole series of chess games, sometimes four or five at a time. Lauren had usually won. Lauren liked to win.

Lester Pig had answered her ad on the Net when Lauren had decided to spread her chess-playing wings. Unfortunately, she had been beaten every time so far.

'But I'm not giving up!' Lauren said with grim determination as she set up the reply screen to accept another defeat. 'I'm going to beat that Lester Pig if it's the last thing I do!'

'That's the spirit,' her gran said. 'Never say die!'

Too right! Lauren thought as she tapped her e-mail message to Lester Pig. *I'm gonna get you, Lester Pig! You see if I don't!*

CHAPTER 2

Abbey School, Portsmouth. 4.10 p.m.

Tamsyn, Rob and Josh were in the computer club room after lessons had ended, keen to discover what had gone wrong with the computers earlier in the day. The spider shape was locked onto every computer screen in the entire school. Sometimes, as with Tamsyn's screen, it was really obvious – sometimes not. But once a person knew what they were looking for, a leg or section of abdomen or whatever could always be distinguished.

The system crash had been the talk of the school that day. Some pupils – Josh and Rob and Tamsyn, for instance – were annoyed at the disruption and puzzled by exactly what had happened. Others enjoyed the brief holiday it afforded them from computer-based lessons, without caring who their mysterious benefactor was.

Mr Findlay had telephoned the company who networked Abbey's computers: an offshoot of the PRIME organization, called PRIMEWORKS. As they had originally linked all the school's computers together, it was up to them, Mr Findlay said, to sort out this problem which had caused so much disruption. And sort it out pronto, too!

It was PRIME who gave access to the World Wide Web and the Internet and who bridged the gap between the school computers and the phoneline and the Net.

The school had subscribed to PRIME because their service centre, the company called PRIME-WORKS, was locally based.

The three friends looked on as two PRIME-WORKS employees checked things out.

'I knew Josh would be to blame,' Rob said with a grin.

'Excuse me!' Josh said. 'Just because the virus was found on the computer I was using, doesn't mean it was my fault.' He looked at one of the women from PRIMEWORKS. 'Does it?'

Karen Williams swallowed a mouthful of sandwich and shook her head. She was a large, outgoing, talkative woman in her early twenties. From what they could make out, her briefcase seemed to be entirely filled with sandwiches. She was constantly eating.

Karen Williams sat on a desk and chattered to the three of them. Her colleague, a quiet, mousy young woman in her late teens, had taken over the work after an initial burst of skilled activity from Karen.

'This was a pretty sophisticated piece of business,' Karen said. 'It was a Boot sector stealth virus.

Things like that are called Trojans, and this particular Trojan was also a time bomb. Someone with a
lot of know-how landed this lot in your laps.'

'Not Josh, then, obviously,' Tamsyn said, smil-
ing at Rob.

'Hey!' Josh was offended. 'I reckon I could
plant a virus if I felt like doing something that
stupid.'

'Aha!' Karen pointed a finger at him. 'So,
you're confessing, eh?'

'What?' Josh looked quite shocked. 'Of course
not! I wouldn't do some petty piece of vandalism
like that.'

Karen grinned. 'Just kidding,' she said.

'So why did it go off when it did?' Rob asked.

'Interesting question,' Karen said, opening her
briefcase and plucking out another triangle
of sandwich. 'We think it was date and time
controlled. You know, set up to trigger today …'
she wiggled her eyebrows, 'when the clock struck
noon.' The rest of what she said was half-muffled
by food, but audible. 'Of course, you were lucky.
It was only a mild virus. I mean, really mild. All
it did was clog up your system. We'll have
you up and running in no time.' She glanced
over her shoulder to where her colleague was
working at Josh's screen. 'Won't we, Babs?'

'Mm.'

'Quiet type,' she said with a wink. 'But she
knows what she's doing. One of the best.'

'So, how did the virus get into our computers?'
asked Tamsyn.

'Someone put it there,' Karen said. 'It was probably imported in on a diskette, or downloaded from another program.'

'What? Today, you mean?' asked Josh.

Karen shrugged. 'Not necessarily,' she said. 'It could have been lurking there for a while. Trojans can be like that. And then once it's triggered – wham! Off it goes, from computer to computer, like a nasty cold going through a class of school kids. That's why these things are called viruses.'

At that moment Mr Findlay arrived, fresh from trying to explain the situation to the head teacher.

He looked hopefully at Karen. 'Well? Any luck?'

'Yeah, we found it,' Karen replied.

Karen explained the nature of their discoveries to Mr Findlay. 'Of course,' she said, 'if this had been a proper *killer* virus, things would have been a little different. Your hard disk could have been completely mashed. Your entire filing system could have been wiped. In short, you could have been in a real pickle, Jack.'

Mr Findlay winced at this use of his first name. He glanced over at the other PRIMEWORKS employee. Tamsyn saw a brief frown gather on his face and then disappear, as though a thought had flitted through his brain for an instant.

'So,' he said, 'no real damage done, hmm?'

Karen shook her head. 'We'll install an updated virus checker to be on the safe side. You'll still be open to attack until we discover the nature of this virus,' she said. 'But viruses like this are usually pretty random in who they hit. I think you've just been unlucky.'

'What kind of person would do something like this?' Tamsyn asked. 'I mean, OK, you said it was sophisticated, but the way I see it, the effect is about as sophisticated as lobbing a brick through someone's window just for the sake of it. I mean, it's just petty-minded vandalism, isn't it?'

'Too right,' Josh said. 'I reckon it's the work of some sad, lonely little nerdling with no kind of life at all.'

Karen burst out laughing, liberally spraying Mr Findlay with half-chewed sandwich. 'Nice one!' she said. 'Oops, sorry, Jack.'

Mr Findlay gave her an expressive look as he brushed egg and cress away from his jacket.

'You know something,' Rob said, 'I reckon we ought to find this virus-twerp.' He gestured towards the computers. 'I mean, we've solved things a lot more complicated with the Internet in the past. What say we get down to it and use our computer knowhow to dig up this slimy little worm ourselves?'

'Use a computer to catch a computer-pest,' Tamsyn said. 'I like it.'

'Great idea,' Josh said. 'This virus-toad is just bound to be an utter dork. He probably spends most of his time counting the hairs on the palms of his hands. We'll winkle him out and expose him in no time flat!'

'You may not find it all that easy,' Karen said. 'He may be reckless, but he knows what

he's doing, trust me. You may need some expert
help.'

Rob smiled. 'I was just thinking the same thing
myself,' he said. He looked at Tamsyn and Josh.
'How about coming back to my place to summon
up some *expert* help?' He grinned. 'From Tom,
Mitch and Lauren!'

Manor House, Portsmouth. 5.45pm.

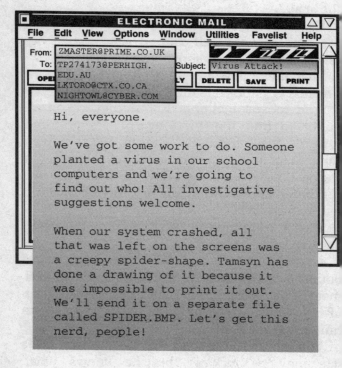

```
┌─────────────────────────────────────────────────┐
│ ■            ELECTRONIC MAIL              △ ▽    │
│ File  Edit  View  Options  Window  Utilities  Favelist  Help │
│ From: ZMASTER@PRIME.CO.UK                        │
│ To:   TP274173@PERHIGH.    Subject: Virus Attack!│
│ OPE   EDU.AU               Y   DELETE  SAVE  PRINT│
│       LKTORO@CTX.CO.CA                            │
│       NIGHTOWL@CYBER.COM                          │
│                                                  │
│     Hi, everyone.                                │
│                                                  │
│     We've got some work to do. Someone           │
│     planted a virus in our school                │
│     computers and we're going to                 │
│     find out who! All investigative              │
│     suggestions welcome.                         │
│                                                  │
│     When our system crashed, all                 │
│     that was left on the screens was             │
│     a creepy spider-shape. Tamsyn has            │
│     done a drawing of it because it              │
│     was impossible to print it out.              │
│     We'll send it on a separate file             │
│     called SPIDER.BMP. Let's get this            │
│     nerd, people!                                │
└─────────────────────────────────────────────────┘
```

Rob went on to explain the exact nature of the attack in greater detail while Josh and Tamsyn breathed down his neck.

They had scanned the drawing of the spider and it was already filed in the computer, waiting to be sent. Tamsyn had been careful to make her drawing as similar to the shape on her screen as possible. At this stage in their search, any detail might prove to be a vital clue in tracking down the attacker.

'Hey, wait a minute,' Tamsyn said, as she re-read Rob's e-mail. 'You've put Tom's ID code at his school. He's got a computer at home, now, remember?'

Rob glanced at her. 'Well spotted,' he said. 'That was a deliberate mistake to check you were paying attention.'

'Yeah, *right*,' Tamsyn said drily as Rob went back to the top of the screen and altered Tom's code to read:

```
SHERLOCK@BIGDOMAIN.AU
```

Rob signed the note and clicked on the SEND button.

Karen Williams had said they might need expert help to unearth the virus attacker. Well, what better expert help could they possibly call on than the three people who had helped them solve so many mysteries in the past?

Within seconds their e-mail message was

waiting to be read across the other side of the world in New York, Toronto and Perth.

Perth, Australia.
Tuesday 15th October, 8.00 a.m.

'Hey, boys!' Mrs Peterson's voice rang out from the kitchen. 'I won't tell you again! Breakfast!'

'Five minutes, honey,' Mr Peterson hollered back, not even glancing away from the screen as his thirteen-year-old son navigated his way expertly through the Internet system.

They were in search of locations for their summer holiday. The Net held so much holiday information that they almost didn't know where to begin. Everywhere from Ayers Rock to Zanzibar.

Tom grinned at his father, his eyes glowing with pleasure. At last! A computer in his own home linked to the Internet. No more squeezing time in on the only school computer for him. Now he could really score some serious surfing time! His father had been promising to buy a home computer for some time – for so long, in fact, that Tom had begun to doubt that the thing would ever actually appear.

But that weekend they had gone to a specialist computer store in the city and had come back with several boxes full of equipment. A whole lot of time spent poring over manuals later, the system was set up and online. From then on, all their spare time had been spent surfing the Net together and battling for the best seat in front of the screen.

Tom had e-mailed all his friends with the brilliant news immediately. Meanwhile, Tom's mother was feeling like a computer widow. The only time she saw her husband or her son was when they zipped into the kitchen to raid the fridge. So far as she could tell, they'd both gone Internet-crazy!

Tom's father tapped his son's shoulder and pointed to a small panel at the bottom right of the screen. ELECTRONIC MAIL: 1 MESSAGE WAITING.

'How long has that been there?' Tom wondered aloud.

'Beats me,' his father said, whipping the mouse out of Tom's hand and double-clicking over the underlined name *Vanuatu* on the screen menu. Mr Peterson rather fancied the idea of a vacation on an exotic Pacific island!

New information filled the screen with glowing south-seas colours.

'Hey, Dad, can I read my mail?' Tom said.

'Who says it's for you, mate?' Mr Peterson said. 'It's just possible it might be a message for me, y'know.'

'Five dollars says it isn't.'

'You're on!'

A few seconds later Rob's e-mail filled the screen.

Tom laughed. 'That's five dollars you owe me,

Dad. I knew it was for me – we're logged in on my ID!'

Mr Peterson scrambled his hand through his son's hair. 'No probs, Tom, m'boy. I don't mind owing you five dollars.' He stood up and strolled out of the den. 'In fact,' he said, 'I don't mind owing it to you for the next twenty years. Now, c'mon, let's leave the computer for a while, son, and go and eat breakfast before your mother starts spitting spanners.'

'Five minutes, Dad,' Tom said.

Two minutes later, Tom was watching as Tamsyn's spider drawing oozed out of the printer.

'Well, well,' Tom said to himself. 'I think I may be able to help you guys out a little here. I've met one of these fellows face to face!' In no time at all he was back at the net menu and the arrow-shaped cursor was hovering over EDUCATION. Several clicks of the mouse and a number of screens later, Tom was looking at the particular file he wanted.

Now all that he needed to do was to e-mail Rob and tell him the Net address of the file he had found.

CHAPTER 3

Manor House, Portsmouth. 7.26 a.m.

Rob booted up his computer first thing on Tuesday morning to check if anybody had replied to his note from the previous evening.

One message awaited him. It was from Tom in Perth. Rob opened it up.

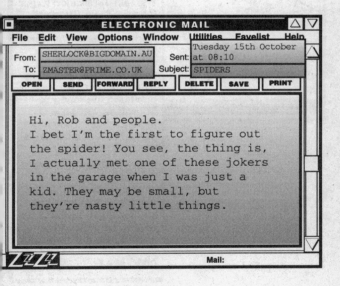

ELECTRONIC MAIL △ ▽

File Edit View Options Window Utilities Favelist Help

From: SHERLOCK@BIGDOMAIN.AU   Sent: Tuesday 15th October at 08:10
To: ZMASTER@PRIME.CO.UK   Subject: SPIDERS

OPEN   SEND   FORWARD   REPLY   DELETE   SAVE   PRINT

Hi, Rob and people.
I bet I'm the first to figure out
the spider! You see, the thing is,
I actually met one of these jokers
in the garage when I was just a
kid. They may be small, but
they're nasty little things.

Mail:

Tom went on to give the address of the Web Site which he thought Rob and the others might find helpful.

Rob made a note of it. It was one of a whole series of Wildlife Files on an education web site called Wonders of the Animal Kingdom, sponsored by one of the big Australian museums.

NET NAVIGATOR

File   Edit   View   Options   Window   Utilities   Favelist   Help

Previous   Next   Home   Print

BLACK WIDOW SPIDER

MALE

FEMALE

BLACK WIDOW SPIDER

The black widow's name refers to the infamous reputation that the female has of eating the male after he has fertilized her. The female is much larger than the male. They are found throughout the warmer parts of the world and often travel to new locations in cargoes of fruit, etc. They are known by a variety of names, including the redback, hourglass, button and jockey spider. They have powerful venom which is deadly to their prey.

A shy, solitary creature, the black widow will attack humans if disturbed, by secreting a venom which assaults the nervous system, causing severe pain and muscular cramps as well as causing breathing difficulties.

'Charming little chap,' Rob muttered to himself as he scrolled the continuing information down his screen. But he could see what Tom had been getting at in his e-mail. Tamsyn's drawing of the spider from the virus-attacked screens at Abbey School did look remarkably similar to the illustration of the female black widow on this file.

Rob printed out all four pages from this section of the site.

Something played on his mind as he watched the paper slide smoothly out of his printer. Something that Karen Williams had said about viruses being random. If the attack had been set up to trap anyone who walked into it, without the attacker caring who was caught, then the chances were that they would never find the culprit.

On the other hand, if someone had deliberately targeted the Abbey – well, then motives, means and methods could be figured out and the attacker may well be hauled out from whatever rock he was hiding under. If it was a he.

Rob picked up the page with the illustrations of the spiders on it. The male and female were completely different shapes, and judging from the bloated abdomen in Tamsyn's drawing, the spider in question was undoubtedly a she.

Very interesting, he thought.

'Josh! You'll be late for school if you don't get your skates on!' Mrs Allan called up the stairs. She ducked back as Josh came half-sliding down the banisters with his school bag over his shoulder.

'It's all under control, Mum,' he said as he landed in the hall. 'Split-second timing is my speciality.'

'Wringing your neck will be my speciality if you break those banisters with your acrobatics!' Mrs Allan said with a laugh as she went back into the kitchen.

Whistling tunelessly through his teeth, Josh headed for the front door. There was some post on the mat. He flicked through the brown envelopes before dumping them on the side cabinet. Bills.

'See you later,' he called as he opened the front door and stepped outside.

'Hello, what's this, then?' he muttered.

A large padded brown envelope had been tucked precariously through the handle of the letter box. He plucked it out, wondering why the postie hadn't rung the bell. She usually did when things wouldn't go through the door.

The envelope was addressed to him. Whoh! Unexpected goodies. Great. Josh pulled the door closed and walked down the path. He noticed that there was no postmark on the envelope – neither was there a stamp. Odd.

Inside the envelope was a magazine. For a moment, Josh assumed it must be a computer magazine, possibly ordered for him by his parents. His bedroom floor was awash with such magazines, but there was always space for more.

The boggle-eyed face of a hare stared at him from the front cover, head tilted and ears standing up like furry surfboards. 'WILDLIFE WONDERWORLD' read the masthead on the magazine.

'Eh?' Josh stared at the wildlife magazine. Why should he be sent an animal magazine? If anyone was into animals, it was Tamsyn, not him. He couldn't tell a wildebeest from a wombat.

And then Josh noticed that a computer diskette was taped to the front of the magazine.

The sleeve that protected the diskette was striped black and white and printed with the words:

> *ARACHNIDS ANONYMOUS:*
> *EVERYTHING YOU ALWAYS WANTED*
> *TO KNOW BUT WERE AFRAID TO ASK.*
> *THE LATEST GRAPHICS! QUALITY*
> *SOUNDS! PC COMPATIBLE.*

While Josh was puzzling over who could have sent him the magazine, his bus swept past. Rats! Now he was going to get to school too late for an early-morning surf of the Net.

He tore the free diskette off the front of the magazine and stuffed it in his pocket.

Who knows, there might be something

interesting on it? And if not, he could always give it to Tamsyn. She might even know what an arachnid was.

He zipped the magazine up in his bag, and then began the trek to school.

Abbey School. 9.10 a.m.

'Hey, Tammy,' Josh called as he burst through the double swing doors of the Technology Block. 'I've got something here you might be interested in.'

Tamsyn frowned over her shoulder at him as she made her way along the bustling corridor-full of students towards the form room. 'Don't call me Tammy,' she shouted. 'It's an extremely annoying habit that you've picked up!'

She sped up as the grinning Josh followed her.

'Hey, do you know what an arch-nid is?' he called after her.

'What a what is?' she yelled back

'Arch-nid?' Josh called. 'Arch-noid? Arack-oid?' He fumbled in his pocket for the diskette. 'It's some sort of animal, I think. I've been sent a free diskette through the post, and it's— Hey, Tam! Wait for me!'

Tamsyn wasn't listening any more and she banged her way into the girls' cloakroom, slamming the door in his face.

'Well, I'll just have to take a look at it all by myself at lunchtime,' Josh called through the door. 'Huh! Some people!'

Josh shrugged. Someone wasn't in the best of moods today, obviously. Well, if she was going to be like that about it, he'd just keep the diskette all to himself until he had the time to run it on the computer at lunch break.

Inside the cloakroom, Tamsyn stood in front of a mirror tidying her appearance before the start of lessons. She needed a breather too.

Her short fuse that morning was nothing to do with Josh, although she really *didn't* like being called 'Tammy'. She was irritated because her younger brother Nick was in one of his practical joke moods. He had hidden some post that had come for her and had refused to tell her where it was unless she paid him for the information.

She'd said 'no way' and he'd run off to catch his school bus without telling her the hiding place. Later that afternoon, she'd have the pleasure of killing Nick, of course, but right then she had to content herself with snapping at Josh.

After all, it wasn't every day that Tamsyn received padded brown envelopes through the post, even though she only caught a glimpse of it before Nick spirited it away with a shriek of aggravating laughter.

A plump little envelope. The sort of envelope a cassette or something of a similar size might be sent in. Except that Tamsyn hadn't ordered anything like that. So, the question was: what was in it?

CHAPTER 4

Perth, Australia. 4.15 p.m.

Tom had been gathering information for his Crime Collection for some time. His father was a detective with the Perth police force and Tom had similar aspirations.

Items such as newspaper cuttings and physical objects were kept in a special drawer in his bedroom; other details were stored on a special computer file which Tom updated regularly.

Some time ago, Tom had found a useful section on the Internet: a CRIME section, subdivided into a lot of very interesting files. There were subsections of fingerprints, DNA testing and photo-fit pictures, and it was one of these files that was holding Tom's attention that afternoon. A section on CRIMINAL PROFILING was up on his screen.

Previous | Next | Home | Print

'That's just what I wanted,' Tom muttered to himself as he scrolled the screen up to read the lengthy details of how such a profile could be built up. He scribbled notes as he went along. He might be on the other side of the world from where the crime had taken place, but via the Internet, he could help his friends out even further.

Using the techniques outlined on this file, Tom was certain he would be able to give Rob and the others a really good idea of the type of person they were looking for.

Tamsyn had calmed down a little about her pesky brother during the morning. Now she was only simmering. Nick wouldn't be killed after all – just beaten to a squishy pulp.

She was sitting in the school common room with its ring of wooden benches and drinks and snack machines.

Rob came over with a couple of soft drinks.

He handed Tamsyn the four-page printout of Tom's Black Widow file. Punctuating her reading with slurps from the can, Tamsyn made her way through the document.

'Well, I agree the female spider does look a lot like the one on my screen yesterday,' Tamsyn said. 'But I don't see how all the rest of this helps us very much.' She smiled. 'Unless Tom thinks we've been attacked by a huge, mutant, super intelligent spider-creature.' She glanced at the last page. 'I mean – does it really help to know the official Latin name?' She stared at the double-barrelled name. It was about a metre long and totally unpronounceable!

'Probably not,' Rob agreed. 'But I think I'll send copies of this to Lauren and Mitch, just in case they can come up with something. And at least it means we can give the attacker a name.'

'Black Widow, you mean?' Tamsyn said. She looked up at Rob. 'Do you think it's a woman?'

'The shape on the screen was the female of the

species,' Rob said. 'See? Its abdomen is much larger than the male's.'

'I know how it feels,' Tamsyn joked, turning back to the first page. Two words caught her attention. *Class: Arachnida*.

'What is it?' Rob asked as he saw the frown gather on Tamsyn's brow.

'Josh was yelling at me this morning about a diskette he'd been given to do with archnids, or something like that. I wonder if he meant arachnids. I mean, the proper name for spiders is arachnids.' She looked at Rob. 'He was asking if I knew what the word meant – he said it was something to do with animals.'

'I don't follow you,' Rob said. 'Josh told you he was given a diskette? Who gave it to him?'

'I don't know,' Tamsyn admitted. 'I wasn't really paying much attention. He said it came through the post, I think.'

'It's a bit of a coincidence, don't you think? It could be a set-up!' Rob exclaimed. 'Where's Josh now?'

'In the Tech. Block, I suppose. But I don't see—'

'We've got to stop him using that diskette!' Rob said. 'It could be from the Black Widow!'

'But how …?'

Rob wasn't waiting around to chat about it. He was already speeding along the corridor, skilfully managing to avoid skittling innocent bystanders in his rush to prevent Josh from falling into what could be a Black Widow trap.

Computer Club, Abbey School. 12.14 p.m.

Josh slid the diskette out of its protective card cover and inserted it into the computer.

He nearly jumped clear out of his seat as the door behind him came crashing open. Something whacked into the back of his chair and an arm snaked over his shoulder.

'Eyyoww!' Josh yelled as he was sent flying. 'What kind of a raving maniac— Rob! Rob? What the heck—' Josh gaped as Rob ejected the diskette from the machine.

Tamsyn arrived breathlessly in the doorway.

'Did you stop him?' she gasped.

Rob tossed the diskette and caught it in his fist. 'In the nick of time!' he said. He looked at Josh, who was busy untangling himself from his upended chair. 'Don't you know what an arachnid is, Josh? It's a spider!'

Josh was about to say something when the full meaning of Rob's words hit him. He sat there on the floor with his mouth hanging open.

'Now then, what's all this noise about?' They all looked around. Mr Findlay was looming over Tamsyn in the doorway. 'Josh? Rob? What's going on? You know I won't have horseplay in here.'

Josh stood up. 'I've just been set up, sir!' he exclaimed angrily. He pointed to the diskette in Rob's hand. 'I got that in the post this morning.'

'Explain,' Mr Findlay said impatiently.

'It's about arachnids, sir,' Rob said, brandishing the printed card cover at Mr Findlay. 'Arachnids are spiders.'

Mr Findlay looked puzzled. 'Your point being?'

Josh explained the odd circumstances in which he'd received the diskette. 'Our computers are hit by a virus which leaves a spider on the screen,' Josh continued. 'And the very next day I get a surprise free gift of a disk all about spiders.'

'Are you suggesting that the person who caused the virus is targeting you?' Mr Findlay asked. His eyes narrowed. 'If this is some stupid private feud that has spilled over to involve the school, Josh, then I think you'd better tell me all about it right now.'

'It isn't, sir,' said Josh. 'Honest – I haven't got a clue what's going on.'

'But we can help you solve the mystery, Mr Findlay,' Rob added. 'We've already got some friends helping us, and we reckon that if we—'

'Yes, thank you, Rob.' Mr Findlay interrupted. 'But I don't think a whole posse of teenagers ramp-aging about the place is going to help matters very much.' He stalked over and took the diskette out of Rob's hand.

'This is going straight over to the people at PRIMEWORKS,' he said. 'They're the experts. They'll be able to check if it really is infected.' He frowned at Josh.

'We'd like to help,' Tamsyn said.

Mr Findlay waved a dismissive hand at her. 'Not necessary,' he said. 'And for the time being, some new rules. I think it would be for the best if you confine your computer activities to reading data rather than using programs, OK? We don't want any more disasters.'

With that, Mr Findlay swept out of the room.

'He thinks it's all my fault!' Josh said.

Rob frowned. 'Then we'd better get to work to prove him wrong.'

'If he *is* wrong,' Tamsyn said.

Josh stared at her in disbelief.

She held her hands up. 'I don't mean I think you're to blame,' she said. 'But we've got to face the fact that Black Widow has sent a diskette to your house, Josh. Maybe someone really is out to get you.'

'OK,' Rob said. 'We've got three clues so far.' He counted on his fingers. 'One, Black Widow must have, or have had, access to the school – the virus needed to be physically put into the system, right? Two, Black Widow knows Josh's address.'

'And three?' Josh asked.

Rob looked from Tamsyn to Josh. 'We're looking for someone who likes the idea of being called Black Widow.'

'A weirdo, then,' Tamsyn said. 'A full-time, dangerous, big-bottomed weirdo!'

Toronto. 7.20 a.m.
Still in her pyjamas, Lauren sat in front of her computer. She was keen to check out what Lester Pig had made of her last chess move the night

before. It had been a peach, even if she had to say it herself. Finally, it looked like Lauren had Lester Pig on the ropes. Three more moves, Lauren figured, and she'd win – if everything went according to plan.

'Yesss!' The e-mail panel showed one message waiting. It might be another message from Rob and the others at Abbey School though. Lauren had already read their first call for help to find the virus attacker, but she hadn't had much time to think about it. She was far too busy battling Lester Pig to the death!

She tapped OPEN and the e-mail appeared. It was from Lester Pig. Lauren read the note in silence.

'Arrrgh!'

'Don't tell me,' said her gran as she walked through in her dressing gown on her way to the bathroom. 'Is it from Lucy Dog?'

'Lester Pig!'

'Whatever. Bad news, honey?'

Lauren stared venomously at the screen, then at the chess set that stood at the side of her computer. She imagined the suggested move. Lester Pig's queen had come swooping right across the board like a Scud missile – seemingly out of nowhere. Lauren was in check. All her plans had fallen to pieces.

She took a few calming breaths. 'OK,' she said softly to herself. 'Don't blow a fuse, here. You haven't lost yet. You can get out of this. Don't panic.'

Her gran peered briefly over her shoulder at the game board. 'Hey, you want to watch the queen there, honey. You'll be in check if you don't keep an eye out.'

'Thanks, Allie,' Lauren sighed. 'You might have mentioned it a little earlier!'

Her gran chuckled. 'How could I?' she said. 'I only just got up.' She patted Lauren's shoulder. 'Keep plugging away, honey.'

Her gran disappeared into the bathroom. Lauren just wasn't in the mood to try and figure out her next move.

Instead, she pulled Rob's e-mail out of store and read it through again. She needed to focus on something else. Maybe here was a problem she could make some headway with. A thought struck her and she decided to send an e-mail back. She quickly calculated the time in the UK. It would be about half past twelve, midday. Rob and the others would be at school.

She clicked to an e-mail screen and began to type.

CHAPTER 5

Abbey School. 12.40 p.m.

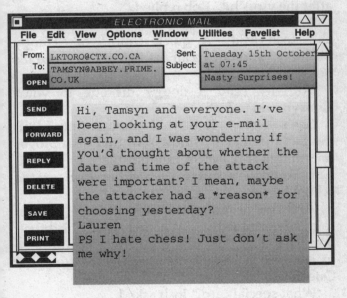

ELECTRONIC MAIL

File   Edit   View   Options   Window   Utilities   Favelist   Help

From: LKTORO@CTX.CO.CA
To: TAMSYN@ABBEY.PRIME.CO.UK
OPEN

Sent: Tuesday 15th October at 07:45
Subject: Nasty Surprises!

SEND
FORWARD
REPLY
DELETE
SAVE
PRINT

Hi, Tamsyn and everyone. I've been looking at your e-mail again, and I was wondering if you'd thought about whether the date and time of the attack were important? I mean, maybe the attacker had a *reason* for choosing yesterday?
Lauren
PS I hate chess! Just don't ask me why!

Josh pointed to the PS and smiled. 'I bet you I know what that's all about,' he said. 'She's found some chess-whizz on the Net and she's getting walloped all over the place!'

'She might have a point about the date, though,' Tamsyn said. 'The 14th of October.' She looked at her two friends. 'Does that mean anything to either of you?'

'What? Apart from it being Mr Findlay's birthday?' Rob asked.

'It was?' Josh said. 'How do you know that?'

'Because he made some comment about it when he came galloping in here yesterday, just after the virus hit,' Rob replied.

'You think the virus was a birthday present, eh?' Josh said. 'A quick chorus of "Happy Birthday" and out go all the lights. I suppose it's possible.'

'So why send a dodgy diskette to you?' Tamsyn said to Josh.

'She's right,' Rob said thoughtfully. 'But the fact that Black Widow sent that disk proves one thing. This isn't a random piece of vandalism. Someone's out to get either Josh or the school.'

'And we're going to stop them,' Tamsyn said determinedly. 'Whether the birthday-boy likes it or not.' She grinned. 'Hey, I'll have to ask him if he got his special card from the Queen.'

'What special card?' Josh asked.

Tamsyn laughed. 'Didn't you know? Everyone gets a card from the Queen on their hundredth birthday!'

One further message awaited their attention.

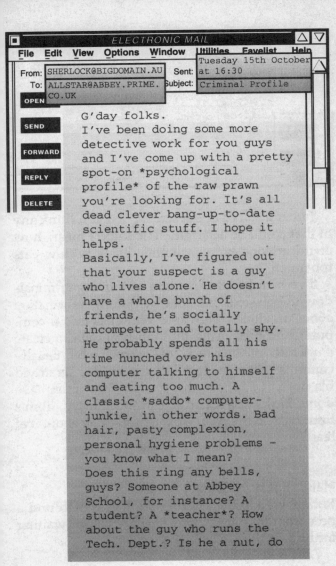

File   Edit   View   Options   Window   Utilities   Favelist   Help

From: SHERLOCK@BIGDOMAIN.AU   Sent: Tuesday 15th October at 16:30
To: ALLSTAR@ABBEY.PRIME.CO.UK   Subject: Criminal Profile

OPEN
SEND
FORWARD
REPLY
DELETE

G'day folks.
I've been doing some more
detective work for you guys
and I've come up with a pretty
spot-on *psychological
profile* of the raw prawn
you're looking for. It's all
dead clever bang-up-to-date
scientific stuff. I hope it
helps.
Basically, I've figured out
that your suspect is a guy
who lives alone. He doesn't
have a whole bunch of
friends, he's socially
incompetent and totally shy.
He probably spends all his
time hunched over his
computer talking to himself
and eating too much. A
classic *saddo* computer-
junkie, in other words. Bad
hair, pasty complexion,
personal hygiene problems –
you know what I mean?
Does this ring any bells,
guys? Someone at Abbey
School, for instance? A
student? A *teacher*? How
about the guy who runs the
Tech. Dept.? Is he a nut, do

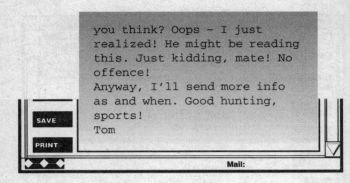

```
you think? Oops - I just
realized! He might be reading
this. Just kidding, mate! No
offence!
Anyway, I'll send more info
as and when. Good hunting,
sports!
Tom
```

SAVE

PRINT

◆ ◆ ◆   Mail:

Tamsyn stared at the screen. 'Do you think any of that could be accurate?' she said. 'I mean, how could anyone know whether Black Widow eats too much?'

'I've heard of this method of hunting criminals down,' Rob said. 'It's done by putting information about previously convicted criminals into a computer, and then using the statistical data to create a picture of the type of person who usually commits particular types of crimes.' He scratched his nose. 'I suppose that's what Tom must have done.' He looked round at Josh and Tamsyn. 'Tom's been right in the past. We ought to think about it at least.'

Manor House. 4.00pm.

Rob arrived home after school that day to find a note from his father and a small envelope waiting for him on the kitchen table.

Rob
*I've only got a second – I dropped this off on my
way to a meeting over in Gosport. It was sent to
us by someone who thought we might like to
employ them. I think it's an example of the kind
of work they can do. Would you take a look at it
for me and report back? It's probably amateurish,
but I wouldn't want to miss out if it's any good.
Dad.*

Rob's parents ran a company called GAME-
ZONE which created new computer games.
Quite often Rob was called on to test-run new
games for them. But he'd never been asked to
check out anything quite like this before. *Mind
you*, he thought, *it makes sense to show a prospective
employer what you're capable of, I suppose.*

Rob tipped the envelope and a diskette slid
out. Written in ballpoint on the sleeve were the
words 'The Hourglass of Horror!' Rob assumed it
must be some sort of new game prototype.

He dropped it into his lap and moved over to
the fridge to get himself a snack to keep him
going until his parents arrived home. Then he
headed for his room.

Rob swigged from a can of Coke as his computer loaded all its relevant software. He inserted
the diskette when it had finished and rested his
hand down on the mouse.

A very ordinary-looking opening page filled
the screen first. Just script on a black background.

Rob wasn't impressed. If things didn't improve pretty quickly, he wasn't even going to bother getting into the game.

He moved the cursor to an hourglass-shaped icon and double-clicked to move the game on.

He nibbled at a pepperoni sausage as the screen changed and a new picture began gradually to appear.

For the first few seconds, Rob couldn't make out what those thin lines might represent. The spokes of a wheel?

And then it became all too clear.

'Oh, no!' Desperately, Rob tried to exit the program. He frantically thrashed about at several keys in front of him. But it was too late. The screen changed with a bright flash and Rob watched in dismay as new words scrolled themselves out against a lurid red background.

NET NAVIGATOR

File   Edit   View   Options   Window   Utilities   Favelist   Help

Previous   Next   Home   Print

Welcome to the hourglass of horror. Which of you will walk into my little web first, I wonder! You all think you're so *very* clever, so I really don't mind who I catch.

Did you really think that little baby virus was the worst I could do? It isn't. Oh, no. Not by a *long* way! In fact, I have a whole brood of babies hidden away in my web. And this is just another one of them.

OK, I'll get to the point. You smug, self-satisfied, big-mouthed kids have behaved very *badly*, and now you're going to be punished.

But I'm a reasonable person, so I'll give you a nice little *game* to play.

A game has to have a purpose, doesn't it! OK, here's your purpose:

My next attack will be a real *killer*, and your task is to try to stop me! You'll fail, of course and I'll enjoy watching you fail.

I am watching you. All the time. Believe it!

Here is your clue:

BIG BANG! – 17101800

The clock is ticking. Tick Tick Tick.

Rob had only just finished running his eyes over the script when the screen blanked out.

His computer had crashed.

CHAPTER 6

Manor House. 5.08 p.m.

Josh and Tamsyn sat disconsolately on Rob's bed. Summoned urgently by phone, they arrived to find Rob still seriously annoyed with himself. His whole system had crashed big time. Rob had the grim feeling that, when the experts took a look, they'd find his hard disk had been severely mutilated by Black Widow's latest attack. Fortunately his files were all backed up on diskette, so the virus hadn't actually destroyed anything of value. But he wouldn't be able to use his computer again until it had been fixed – and that was a major inconvenience.

'I must have the brains of a retarded toothpick!' Rob stormed. 'I mean, I'd only just read that spider file Tom sent us. And what did it tell me, eh?'

'I know,' Tamsyn said. 'The black widow is also known as the hourglass spider. But—'

'And what do I do?' Rob exploded. 'I put a disk into my system called "The Hourglass of Horror!" There must be algae floating out in the harbour with more brains than me!'

'It could have happened to any one of us,' Tamsyn said soothingly. 'Don't beat yourself up about it.'

Rob had given them the gist of what had appeared on the screen just prior to the crash. He'd even had the presence of mind to scribble down the clue while it was still fresh in his mind.

'At least this means Black Widow isn't just after me,' Josh said.

'No, she's after *all* of us,' Tamsyn said.

'And she knows a lot about us,' Rob added grimly. 'Like, for instance, she must know where my parents work. Plus she must have had a pretty good idea that my dad would bring the disk home for me to try out.'

'Unless it's GAMEZONE that Black Widow is really after,' Tamsyn suggested.

'I doubt it,' Rob said. 'They've got state of the art virus checkers over there. They can even signal brand new viruses. No, Black Widow must have known she couldn't launch a successful attack on GAMEZONE.' He looked at Tamsyn and Josh. 'Face it, pals: Black Widow is after us.'

'Just us?' Josh asked. 'I mean, just the three of us? Or maybe it's all of us? Mitch and Tom and Lauren, too. Perhaps someone we had a run-in with in the past has come crawling out of the woodwork to get us?'

'Thanks a bunch for sharing that thought with us, Josh,' Tamsyn said uneasily. She looked at Rob. 'Do you think it's possible?'

'I don't know,' Rob said. 'But I think we need

to warn the others, just in case. First thing in the morning, when we can get on to the school computers.'

'How much do you think Black Widow actually knows about us?' Tamsyn asked. 'You said she was boasting about watching us all the time. Do you think she could be using the Internet to monitor everything we do? Is that possible?'

'It shouldn't be,' Josh said. 'Not without having a password to get into our stuff. But I suppose she could be hacking into the Abbey Network.' He shook his head. 'I don't like this. I don't like this at all.'

New York, USA. 12.10 p.m.
Mitch dumped his cleaning cloth in the sink and headed for the nearest computer. Lunch break at last, and fortunately one of the screens in CyberSnax was free. CyberSnax was a café near Central Park where customers could surf the net while sipping their cappuccino.

Seventeen-year-old Mitch worked as a general dogsbody for the café's owner, Mr Lewin. In exchange for extra hours and ghastly jobs like clearing out blocked drains, Mitch was allowed free access to the Internet on his break periods. Often up to his elbows in congealed fat and grisly stuff like that, Mitch wasn't always sure if that was such a bargain. But as he pressed the globe icon and entered the Net, he knew it was worth it.

A MAIL WAITING message was flashing. Mitch wondered whether it was an update from Rob about that idiot virus attacker. The last Mitch had heard from Portsmouth had been directions to the web site about black widow spiders which had been waiting for him earlier that morning.

But it wasn't from Portsmouth. It was a message left from someone responding to a bulletin message he'd put up in the American Football section of a New York sports site. He'd been looking to chat with anyone who supported his favourite team, the New York Giants.

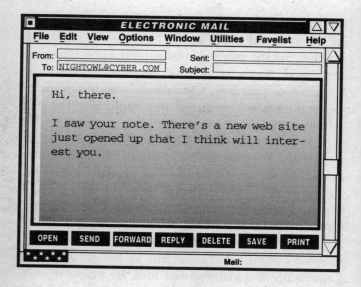

ELECTRONIC MAIL

File   Edit   View   Options   Window   Utilities   Favelist   Help

From:
To: NIGHTOWL@CYBER.COM

Sent:
Subject:

Hi, there.

I saw your note. There's a new web site just opened up that I think will interest you.

OPEN   SEND   FORWARD   REPLY   DELETE   SAVE   PRINT

Mail:

The e-mail went on to give details of the site. It was signed BLACKIE.

Intrigued, Mitch looked up the site.

Mitch navigated the cursor around the screen and clicked on the button to take him to the game.

He tapped his fingers while he waited for the few minutes it took the game to download.

10%. 50%. 80%. 90%. 95%. 99%. Completed.

'Hey, ain't your lunch break over yet, Mitch?' Mr Lewin yelled from behind the counter.

'I only started ten minutes ago,' Mitch called back. He clicked on the RUN icon to start the game.

For a couple of seconds, the burning red shape of a spider filled Mitch's screen. Then glowing red words appeared.

Hey, Mitch, nice to tangle with you!

Yo, Nightowl! Way to crash your computer!

With a gasp, Mitch reached for the mouse. But he was too late. A moment later the screen blacked out.

A yell went up from every computer-using customer in the café.

'Oh, gawd!' Mitch gasped as he stared at the blank black screen in front of him. Every computer in the place had simultaneously gone down.

He whacked his forehead with the heel of his hand.

'Redbacks!' he groaned, suddenly remembering the black widow web site. 'Am I dumb, or what?'

By the time Mr Lewin reached Mitch's station, he found his computer-whizz employee doubled over, banging his head on the table and moaning to himself.

Perth, Australia.
Wednesday 16th October. 7.45 a.m.

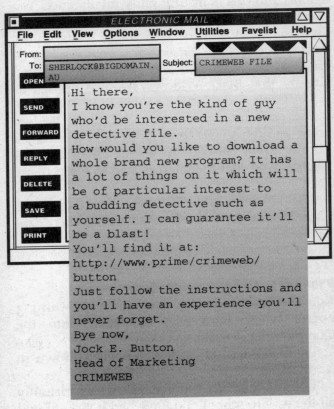

ELECTRONIC MAIL

File   Edit   View   Options   Window   Utilities   Favelist   Help

From:
To: SHERLOCK@BIGDOMAIN.AU   Subject: CRIMEWEB FILE

OPEN

SEND

FORWARD

REPLY

DELETE

SAVE

PRINT

Hi there,
I know you're the kind of guy
who'd be interested in a new
detective file.
How would you like to download a
whole brand new program? It has
a lot of things on it which will
be of particular interest to
a budding detective such as
yourself. I can guarantee it'll
be a blast!
You'll find it at:
http://www.prime/crimeweb/
button
Just follow the instructions and
you'll have an experience you'll
never forget.
Bye now,
Jock E. Button
Head of Marketing
CRIMEWEB

Tom blinked at the e-mail message that he had
just opened. Sure, it was early in the morning and
he was still a little drowsy, but did that Black
Widow jerk really think he was dumb enough to
fall for a blockhead stunt like that?

'I like a challenge as much as the next bloke, mate,' Tom said out loud as he printed out the e-mail. 'But this is insulting my intelligence. You want me to download your program and get sandbagged by a virus! Well, tough boots, chum. And as for Jock E. Button? You've just gotta be kidding me! Like, I'm going to have forgotten already that Black Widows are also known as jockey spiders and button spiders!'

But one thing was certain: if Black Widow knew enough to get through to him, then Black Widow knew enough to get at all of his Net friends. And that meant Tom had to warn them. Fast!

After all, he thought as he typed out an e-mail flash, *they might not all be as attentive as his criminal-busting mind was.*

Abbey School, Portsmouth. 8.45 a.m.

Rob and Josh were just reading Tom's warning e-mail when Tamsyn came racing into the Computer Club room.

She flung a small padded envelope down in front of them.

'Look at that!' she panted. She'd run virtually all the way to school. 'I'd have had it yesterday if my stupid brother hadn't hidden it.'

Rob picked up the envelope. It had Tamsyn's name and address, but no stamp or postmark. He slid out a diskette. Written on the sleeve were the words 'The Hourglass of Horror!'

'That explains the part about her wondering who would get caught first,' Rob said. 'I wonder who else got one of these little time-bombs?'

'She's certainly covering all bases,' Josh said. 'That's me she's targeted, and the two of you – and now Tom. How does she know so much about us? I mean, how did she know Tom was into detective stuff, for instance?'

'Tom?' Tamsyn asked. 'What about Tom?'

Josh pointed to Tom's e-mail on the screen.

'I've got it!' Rob said. 'What happens to old e-mails and stuff like that?'

'Eh? They just go in the recycle bin,' Josh said. 'I keep meaning to clear them out, but I don't get round to it very often. Why?'

'Me too,' Tamsyn added. 'What are you getting at, Rob?'

'We all do the same thing,' Rob explained. 'We've all got stacks of old e-mails and stuff piled up in our recycle bins. So anyone who managed to hack their way into the system could find out plenty of stuff about us just from reading all our old mail!'

'You've got it!' Josh said, snapping his fingers. 'We've all given our addresses at one time or another when we've sent for things through the post.'

'That doesn't explain why she said we were smug and big-mouthed,' Rob said. 'Why big-mouthed? I mean, that sounds like the kind of thing you'd say if you had actually *heard* some-one.'

'You think we're being bugged?' Tamsyn gasped, staring around the lab as if she expected to see a tiny microphone poking out of the wall.

'Let's not get paranoid,' Josh said. 'For a start, no one who heard us chatting could ever accuse us of being smug or big-mouthed, could they?'

'I certainly hope not,' Tamsyn said. She shivered. 'It's just so creepy to think some stranger is keeping tabs on you all the time.'

'If she is,' said Josh. 'She might not be doing it all the time. But I suppose we have to assume she is.'

'I think it's about time we took the initiative,' Rob said. 'Up to now, she's done all the running. I reckon we should start fighting back.'

'What do you recommend?' Josh said drily. 'Insect repellent?'

'Spiders aren't insects,' Tamsyn said. 'What's the plan, Rob?'

'I think we should put a message up on the Abbey School bulletin board in here,' he said, pointing to the computer screen. 'This could be a way of getting a message to her. She might be monitoring it, yeah?'

'Let's hope she reads it,' Tamsyn said.

Rob nodded. 'We need to put something to show we're on to her.'

'Uh, 'scuse me for being a wet blanket,' Josh said, 'but we're not on to her at all.'

'Maybe we're not,' Rob said, taking hold of the mouse and dropping Tom's e-mail off the screen. 'But she doesn't necessarily know that.'

'If she's reading all our mail, she probably *does* know that,' said Josh.

'We'll see,' Rob said.

He clicked up the Bulletin Board screen and began to type.

```
Message for B.W.
Contrary to popular belief, spiders are
much more scared of human beings than
human beings are of spiders.
What are you so scared of?
Oh, by the way, none of your little
time-bombs worked.
```

'What about your one?' Tamsyn asked. 'That worked well enough.'

'I know that,' Rob said. 'And you know that. But if Black Widow is hacking into the school system, then she's not going to know what's going on anywhere else, is she? So let's make her think she's lucked-out all over.'

'Nice one,' chuckled Josh.

```
Why are you doing this? What are you
hoping to achieve? Can we talk it over?
Surely there's some better way of
getting what you want?
Come on, *talk* to us!
Rob Zanelli, Tamsyn Smith and Josh
Allan.
```

'OK,' Rob said, looking round at his two friends. 'Let's see what effect that has.'

CHAPTER 7

Abbey School. 12.30 p.m.

Back in the Computer Club room after a morning of lessons that none of them really paid any attention to, Tamsyn, Rob and Josh were hoping for some response from Black Widow.

There was nothing.

'It's strange we haven't heard anything from Mitch recently,' Josh said. 'Maybe we should e-mail him to check he's OK.'

While Rob tapped out a brief message to their American friend, Tamsyn sat on one of the nearby desks, chewing the end of a pen and frowning down at the clue that Black Widow had given them seconds before Rob's computer had crashed.

THE BIG BANG! 17101800

Josh sat next to her and read over her shoulder.

'The Big Bang must be the killer virus she intends to plant,' he said. 'The numbers might be letters. You know: 1 means A. 7 means, um … G.'

'And zero?'

'Together with the 1, it could make 10. J.' Josh said. 'There you go: A, G, J, A, H … Oh, rats! That leaves two noughts at the end.'

'Brilliant theory number one goes down in flames,' Rob said as he sent Mitch the e-mail. 'Not that the word "agjah" would have clarified things much, anyhow.'

'Wait a minute,' Tamsyn said. 'What if it's another date? Remember Karen said that other virus was date-triggered?'

'Yes,' Rob said thoughtfully. 'Triggered to go off on the date of Mr Findlay's birthday.'

'That's right,' Josh said. 'An anniversary. Might the second virus be planned for another anniversary? But what? If the Big Bang is date-triggered as well, then the 17 could be the day, the 10 could be the month. That would make the 17th of October.'

'That's tomorrow!' Tamsyn almost yelled.

'Hold on,' Josh said. 'The seventeenth of October 1800? What's she done – sent the virus back through time?'

'Time!' Tamsyn shrieked. '1800. On a twenty-four hour clock, 1800 is six o'clock in the evening.'

'So, if you've got it right, the Big Bang is scheduled for six o'clock tomorrow evening,' Rob said. 'That doesn't give us much time.'

'Shouldn't we tell Mr Findlay?' Josh said.

'Especially if the Big Bang is going to happen here.'

'No,' Tamsyn said firmly.

The two boys looked at her.

'First,' Tamsyn explained, 'we offered to help and Mr Findlay turned us down. So I think we should solve this on our own, to prove to him we can. Second, if we tell him something big is going to happen tomorrow evening, all he'll do is close the system down and bring in the PRIMEWORKS people to find the virus.'

'That's what we want, isn't it?' Josh said. 'To stop it.'

'Only partly,' said Rob. 'I know what Tamsyn means. Stopping the Big Bang isn't going to get us any closer to catching Black Widow.'

'Exactly!' Tamsyn said. 'We won't let the Big Bang actually happen. We'll just play for time to catch Black Widow. And catching Black Widow is our priority, right?'

The two boys looked at each other.

'Right!' they chorused.

New York. 9.00 a.m.

Mitch sat at a computer screen in CyberSnax. Somewhere in the background Mr Lewin was still muttering about the computer crash that he had inadvertently caused.

He began to type out an e-mail message to his friends in Portsmouth.

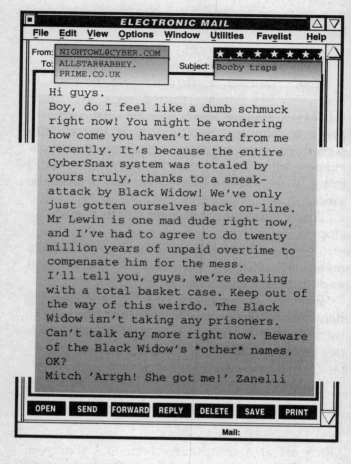

File   Edit   View   Options   Window   Utilities   Favelist   Help

From: NIGHTOWL@CYBER.COM
To: ALLSTAR@ABBEY.PRIME.CO.UK   Subject: Booby traps

Hi guys.
Boy, do I feel like a dumb schmuck
right now! You might be wondering
how come you haven't heard from me
recently. It's because the entire
CyberSnax system was totaled by
yours truly, thanks to a sneak-
attack by Black Widow! We've only
just gotten ourselves back on-line.
Mr Lewin is one mad dude right now,
and I've had to agree to do twenty
million years of unpaid overtime to
compensate him for the mess.
I'll tell you, guys, we're dealing
with a total basket case. Keep out of
the way of this weirdo. The Black
Widow isn't taking any prisoners.
Can't talk any more right now. Beware
of the Black Widow's *other* names,
OK?
Mitch 'Arrgh! She got me!' Zanelli

OPEN   SEND   FORWARD   REPLY   DELETE   SAVE   PRINT

Mail:

Abbey School. 3.45 p.m.

'Black Widow got him as well,' said Josh turning
away from Mitch's e-mail. 'That means Lauren is
the only one of all of us who hasn't been targeted
yet.'

'I've been thinking this through,' Rob said. 'I think Black Widow is just using us to attack the school.'

'Do you think someone at school has upset Black Widow somehow?' asked Tamsyn.

'Could be,' Josh said. 'So, we're looking for someone with a grudge against the school, right?' Josh said. 'Tom suggested that, didn't he? A student or a loony teacher.'

'Hmm, take your pick on the last one!' Tamsyn said. 'Or I suppose it could be an *ex*-student?'

'How about we look up some files and see if anything jumps out at us?' Rob said. 'The entire school roll is on our Web site. And that includes entries about all the staff, plus some ex-staff members and ex-students. You never know, we might turn something up.'

'Yeah,' said Josh. 'Like an ex-teacher called Ms B. Widow.'

Abbey School. 4.00 p.m.

Ex-Abbey Students on the Internet

David Adams	Colin McGilray
Vanessa Arnold	Connie Pasquale
Paul Barrett	Barbara Phelan
Eric Blair	Greg Preston
Ben Brailsford	Tom Price
Rebecca Dando	Mary Vincent
Maria Dawson	Gabrielle Weston
Camilla Ford	David Williams
Anna Hopkins	Barbara Wilde
Lisa Kendall	

The three friends had worked their way through screen after screen of Abbey School information. Bringing up the list of ex-students linked to the Internet was just about their last hope. So far nothing had struck them as even vaguely suspicious.

'Well, that's the closest we've come so far,' Tamsyn said, pointing to one of the names. 'Barbara Wilde.'

Josh looked at her. 'Do you know a lot of spiders called Barbara, then?'

'No, dummy!' Tamsyn said. 'It's the initials. BW. The same as Black Widow. Is there any more information about her, Rob?'

Rob clicked the mouse. 'There you go,' he said, looking at the screen. 'She left the school in October five years ago, and she lives at 24 Larkrise Avenue.'

'October?' Josh said thoughtfully. 'That's mid-term. Does it say why she left?'

'Not on here,' Rob said. 'If there was a special reason, it would probably be on a private file, anyway. And they would be on the school office system, not this one.'

'It's a bit of a coincidence that this Barbara Wilde left in October,' said Tamsyn. 'And our Black Widow starts causing havoc in October. And they've both got the same initials. Worth checking out, do you think?'

'Larkrise Avenue is only a ten minute walk away,' Josh said. 'We could at least find out whether she's still living there.'

'If it is her, you might alert her by doing that. She'd know we were on to her,' Rob said.

'Not if we're dead subtle,' Josh said, standing up.

'I'll come with you,' Tamsyn said. 'I know your idea of dead subtle. "Oi, got any deadly spiders living here, mister?"'

'I'm going to have another quick look through the files on the Abbey site, then I'll e-mail the others with the latest news while I'm waiting for my mum to pick me up,' Rob said as he jotted Barbara Wilde's name and address down.

Abbey School. 4.50 p.m.

Rob sat alone in the Computer Club Room, staring at the message that had been posted up on the electronic bulletin board.

Dear Josh, Rob & Tamsyn,

Contrary to popular belief, not *all* spiders are scared of humans. You shouldn't have upset me, this was *nothing* to do with you. But you were very rude about me, and I really cannot tolerate bad manners, so you needed to be taught a lesson.

You asked why I must cause the BIG BANG! Trust me, I have *good* reasons.

People who meddle in other people's lives must be punished, don't you agree? I am going to punish the person who did a bad thing to me.

The clock is ticking. Can't you hear it?

Tick. Tick. Tick. Tick. Tick.

And don't bother lying to me about my little babies. They weren't all caught. Black Widows can hatch out up to 100 pretty little babies at a time, did you know that! Spiders are *so* clever!

No more clues. Remember – I'm watching every move you make, and if you get too close, I'm afraid I'll have to *bite*.

Listen to the clock. Tick. Tick. Tick.

A shiver ran down Rob's back as he read the message that Black Widow had left for them. Up until that moment, he hadn't really thought about what was going on in their mysterious adversary's mind.

He had good reason to think about it now!

If the creepy tone of that message was anything to go by, Black Widow was a total psycho!

ew York, USA. 4.20 p.m.

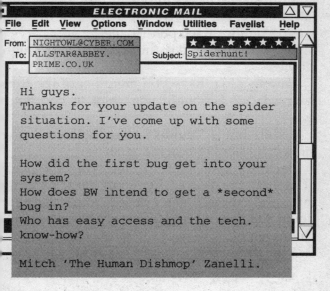

ELECTRONIC MAIL △ ▽

File   Edit   View   Options   Window   Utilities   Favelist   Help

From: NIGHTOWL@CYBER.COM   ★ ★ ★ ★ ★ ★ ★
To: ALLSTAR@ABBEY.   Subject: Spiderhunt!
PRIME.CO.UK

Hi guys.
Thanks for your update on the spider
situation. I've come up with some
questions for you.

How did the first bug get into your
system?
How does BW intend to get a *second*
bug in?
Who has easy access and the tech.
know-how?

Mitch 'The Human Dishmop' Zanelli.

Mitch clicked to send the e-mail across the
cean.

'Hey, Mitch,' Mr Lewin yelled. 'Don't you have
o work to do?'

Mitch sighed. 'Coming,' he called.

Human dishmop was right!

Still, maybe he'd given the guys in Portsmouth something to work on.

Toronto, Canada. 10.50 p.m.

'I give up,' Lauren muttered. 'I completely and utterly give up. I'm never going to play chess again so long as I live.' She lifted the chessboard and tipped the pieces into their box. Lester Pig's latest move had finished the game in a way that was becoming all too predictable.

Her gran appeared in the doorway in her night clothes.

'Lauren King, have you any idea of the time, young lady? I thought you went to bed hours ago.'

'I did, but I couldn't sleep, Allie,' Lauren sighed. 'Lester Pig beat me again.'

'Back to bed, and I'll tell you the story of Robert the Bruce,' her gran said, pattering into the room. She closed the computer down and then swept Lauren out like a hen with chicks.

'Who the what?'

11.20 p.m.

Half an hour later, Lauren was lying wide-eyed in bed, still thinking about Allie's story. Robert the Bruce was an ancient Scottish warrior who, on the brink of defeat, had hidden himself in a cave. He'd watched a spider patiently climb a thread, only to slide down again over and over. The point of the story was that eventually the spider made it to the top of the thread, and, spurred on by the little animal's determination to try, try and try again, Robert the Bruce left the cave, gathered his army back together, and won the war.

Allie had meant it as a pointer to Lauren not to give up, but that wasn't what was keeping her awake. It was something to do with the spider. Something lurking in the back of Lauren's mind. But what?

Lauren slid out of bed and went back to her computer as quiet as the ghost of a mouse.

She found the long Black Widow file that Rob had sent her. There was something in that file. Lauren was certain.

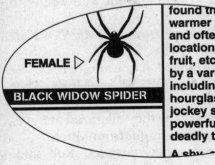

FEMALE ▷

BLACK WIDOW SPIDER

found thro...
warmer parts of th...
and often travel to ne...
locations in cargoes of
fruit, etc. They are known
by a variety of names,
including the redback,
hourglass, button and
jockey spider. They have
powerful venom which...
deadly to their pre...

A shy...

That was it. Jockey spider! Lester Pig could be short for Lester Piggot – a famous jockey! In Rob's last e-mail update, he had wondered why Lauren had been the only one of the Internet Detectives not to be targeted by Black Widow.

Was this the answer?

Was she already unwittingly in contact with Black Widow?

Lauren ran to her gran's room.

'Allie! Allie!' she called, shaking her slumbering gran by the shoulder. 'Wake up! Something real creepy is going on and I don't know what to do about it!'

Abbey School, Portsmouth.
Thursday 17th October, 8.45 a.m.

```
Who has easy access and the tech.
know-how?
```

'What do you think?' asked Rob. 'Who would have access to our system and the know-how to plant the virus?'

'What about someone from PRIMEWORKS?' Tamsyn suggested.

The three friends looked at one another.

'Someone at PRIMEWORKS?' said Josh. 'That could be the answer!'

'Really?' Tamsyn said as they all gazed at the e-mail that had arrived overnight from Mitch.

'Well, we do need a new suspect,' Rob said. 'Now Barbara Wilde is out of the picture.'

Josh and Tamsyn's visit the previous afternoon to Larkrise Avenue had proved a total washout. The new owners of the house had told them that the Wilde family had emigrated to Ireland three years previously.

Admittedly, Ireland wasn't the other side of the world, but, as Josh pointed out when he spoke to Rob later on the phone, it was a heck of a distance to come to hand-deliver those diskettes!

'And the diskettes *were* hand delivered, don't forget,' said Josh.

They needed to look closer to home. It was someone local; someone local and totally out of their tree, if the message Rob showed them first thing that morning was anything to go by.

'What *does* she mean by the Big Bang?' Tamsyn asked as they looked again at the message from Black Widow.

'That's pretty obvious,' Josh said. 'She's got something nasty planned. She sounds like a total fruitcake. All that stuff about us being rude and needing to be taught a lesson.'

'Yeah,' said Rob, 'and that part about punishing people who meddle in other people's lives.'

Tamsyn shuddered. 'That's the creepiest thing I've ever read in my entire life!' she said. 'I mean, this is worse than anything you'd get in a horror film, because this is *real*. Black Widow *really* is out there.'

'Yeah,' Josh muttered. 'And out to get us.'

While they were still pondering this uncomfortable fact, Mr Findlay came in.

'Any news about the disk you sent over to PRIMEWORKS?' Tamsyn asked him.

'Not as yet,' Mr Findlay muttered, obviously looking for something. 'Ah!' He picked up a brown folder. 'There it is,' he said. 'Now at least I'll know what I'm supposed to be teaching this evening.'

'Shouldn't PRIMEWORKS have got back to you by now?' Rob asked again. 'I mean, this is pretty important.'

Mr Findlay looked at him in the way that teachers look when they're thinking about something else.

'I spoke to Ms Williams on the phone,' he said. 'She was certain the virus that clogged up our system was random. She said it was highly unlikely that we were being deliberately attacked, but she agreed to look at that diskette. I put it in the post. They probably haven't even received it yet.'

Mr Findlay walked out with the file under his arm.

'The Big Bang is due to go off at six o'clock this evening, and he put a vital piece of evidence in the post?' Josh said. 'Is he off his nut, or what?'

'He doesn't know about the Big Bang, remember,' Rob said.

'The clock is ticking,' Tamsyn said ominously. 'We'd better hope we come up with something soon. Let's meet up again here at lunchtime.'

They followed the line of her eyes to the wall clock. It was nearly nine o'clock. In another nine hours, unless they came up with something, Big Bang was going to hit!

Toronto. 7.00 a.m.
The previous night, her gran had listened patiently as Lauren had gabbled out her realization that Lester Pig could be the person who was threatening to crash Abbey School's computers.

Swathed in dressing gowns, they had taken a late-night look at the computer. That was when the final piece of evidence indicating her identity – so far as Lauren was concerned – had fallen into place. Lester Pig's e-mail address – traced through the routing information attached to one of her messages – showed the tell-tale UK tag that proved she was based in England. She'd never needed to look at it before. She'd always hit REPLY to messages received from Lester Pig.

The problem was – if, as Rob and the others suspected, Lester Pig was hacking into their computers, how was Lauren to let them know without Lester Pig also finding out? It was a real puzzle.

'Let's sleep on it,' Allie had said. 'We'll be able to think more clearly in the morning, I promise you.'

But the morning had come, and Lauren felt no closer to solving her dilemma than before. If only she had Rob or Josh or Tamsyn's phone number! Then she could have simply called them. But no, she had to get through to them on the Net. And she had to do it quickly and without alerting Lester Pig.

'I have an idea,' Allie said, coming up behind Lauren as she sat staring at the computer screen. 'It came to me in the night.'

'You have?'

Allie grinned as she rested her hands on Lauren's shoulders. 'Now, you just set up an e-post to Rob's school, and type what I tell you.'

'E-*mail*!' Lauren said as she took hold of the mouse and shifted the cursor across the screen. 'What's the plan, Allie?'

'You'll see,' Allie said. 'Now. Type this …'

Abbey School. 12.08 p.m.

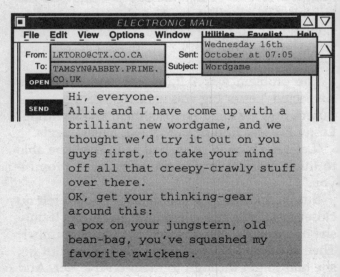

a pox on your jungstern, old
bean-who, you've squashed my
favorite zwickens.
a pox on went jungstern, old
bean-bag, you've squashed up
favorite zwickens.
a pox on your jungstern, the
bean-bag, you've squashed my
favorite zwickens.
a wat er your jungstern, old
bean-bag, spo'ut squashed my
favorite zwickens.
a pox on your jungstern, oLd
bEan-bag, you'Ve Squashed my
favoriTe zwickEns.
a pox on youR jungstern, old
bean-bag, you've squashed my
favorite zwickens.
a Pox on your jungstern, old
bean-bag, you've squashed my
favorIte zwickens.
a pox on your jungstern, old
bean-baG, you've squashed my
favorite zwickens.
@ Pox on your jungstern, old
bean-bag, you've squashed my
favorite zWickens.
a pOx on youR jungstern, old
bean-bag, you've squashed my
favorite zwicKenS..
a pox on your jungstern, old
bean-bag, you've squashed my
favorite zwiCkens.
a pOx.on yoUr jungstern, old
bean-bag, you've squashed my
favourite zwicKens.

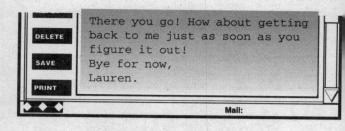

There you go! How about getting
back to me just as soon as you
figure it out!
Bye for now,
Lauren.

DELETE
SAVE
PRINT

Mail:

Rob stared at the bizarre message from Lauren. They were in the middle of a crisis, and she was tinkering with silly word-games? He reached for the mouse to clear the screen.

Josh's hand came down on his. 'Wait a minute,' he said, peering over Rob's shoulder. 'Lauren's pretty sharp. I can't believe she's sent us this just for fun. How about printing it out so we can take a proper look?'

Two minutes later the three of them were staring at a printed sheet of that curious, apparently meaningless message typed out over and over again by their Canadian friend.

'Wait just a minute,' Tamsyn breathed. 'There's something funny going on here.' She took out a red marker pen. 'Some of the words have been changed.' Gradually she worked her way down the page, ringing the hidden message.

```
a pox on your jungstern, old bean-bag,
you've squashed my favorite zwickens.
a pox on your jungstern, old bean-who
you've squashed my favorite zwickens.
a pox on went jungstern, old bean-bag,
```

you've squashed (up) favorite zwickens.
a pox on your jungstern, (the) bean-bag,
you've squashed my favorite zwickens.
a (wat er) your jungstern, old bean-bag,
(spo'ut) squashed my favorite zwickens.
a pox on your jungstern, (o)ld b(E)an-bag,
you've (S)quashed my favori(T)e zwick(E)ns.
a pox on you(R) jungstern, old bean-bag,
you've squashed my favorite zwickens.
a (P)ox on your jungstern, old bean-bag,
you've squashed my favor(I)te zwickens.
a pox on your jungstern, old bean-ba(G)
you've squashed my favorite zwickens.
(d)(P)ox on your jungstern, old bean-bag,
you've squashed my favorite (W)ckens.
a (po)x on you(R) jungstern, old bean-bag,
you've squashed my favorite zwi(cKenS)(.)
a pox on your jungstern, old bean-bag,
you've squashed my favorite zwi(C)kens.
a (po)x(.) on you(U) jungstern, old bean-bag,
you've squashed my favourite zwi(cK)ens.

'Who went up the water spout,' Rob read.
'What does that mean when it's at home?'

'It's the nursery rhyme,' Josh said. 'You know:
Incy-wincy spider went up the water spout,
down came the rain and washed poor Wincy
out.' He poked at the paper. 'She must have
found something out about Black Widow.'

'I think you're right,' Tamsyn said. She looked
around at her friends. 'And I know what. Don't
ask me how ...' she tapped the page with her

pen, 'but Lauren seems to have discovered Black Widow's ID user code. Look!'

Outlined by Tamsyn's pen in the bottom few lines of the script, they could clearly make out an Internet e-mail address spelled out in capital letters and extra full-stops.

LESTERPIG@PWORKS.CO.UK.

Rob's eyes widened. 'Hang on!' he breathed. 'I know that address! I mean, I know where it comes from. Those letters in the middle there are for the PRIMEWORKS office in Portsmouth.'

'But how has Lauren worked it out?' asked Josh.

'I don't know,' said Rob, 'and we certainly can't ask her right now. Do you know what I think? I think it's Karen Williams.'

'Why?' Tamsyn asked.

'It was Karen Williams who networked our system in the first place, don't you remember?' Rob said. 'She could have planted the first virus right then!'

'Yes!' Josh almost shouted. 'And she had the perfect opportunity to plant the Big Bang when she turned up to fix that first problem. And she's female, just like we think Black Widow is. And she eats all the time, which fits Tom's profile. And she tried to deflect Mr Findlay, saying the virus was random.'

'Hold on,' Tamsyn said. 'Tom also said she'd be shy and weird. Karen doesn't come across as being either.'

'Who else can it be?' Josh said. 'I vote we call the cops right now!'

'Hold on a minute,' Tamsyn interrupted. 'I think we need some real proof before we can go anywhere with this theory. The whole point is to trap Black Widow, not to go making wild accusations and ending up looking like prize idiots if we're wrong. Besides, if we *have* got it wrong, and it isn't Karen Williams, all we'll wind up doing is giving the real culprit time to run for cover.'

'OK, so what do you suggest?' Josh asked.

'I don't know,' Tamsyn said. 'Give a person time to think!'

Josh looked at his watch. 'Fine,' he said. 'You've got six hours before the Big Bang.'

'I've got an idea,' Rob said. Josh and Tamsyn turned to look at him. They were desperate for a solution. 'It might just work. But it's going to depend on Lauren.' He moved towards the computer screen.

'OK, Lauren,' he said, his fingers moving rapidly over the keyboard. 'We're all relying on you. Don't let us down!'

CHAPTER 9

Toronto. 7.20 a.m.

Lauren wiped a crescent of milk off her top lip and put her tumbler down. The e-mail from Portsmouth had beeped its presence.

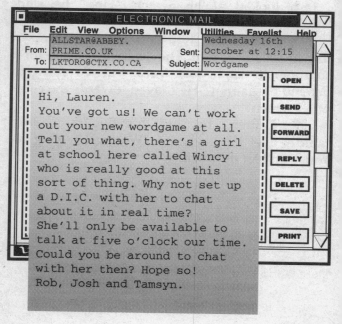

```
ELECTRONIC MAIL

File   Edit   View   Options   Window   Utilities   Favelist   Help

From: ALLSTAR@ABBEY.          Sent: Wednesday 16th
      PRIME.CO.UK                   October at 12:15
  To: LKTORO@CTX.CO.CA     Subject: Wordgame

                                                    OPEN
  Hi, Lauren.
  You've got us! We can't work                      SEND
  out your new wordgame at all.
  Tell you what, there's a girl                     FORWARD
  at school here called Wincy
  who is really good at this                        REPLY
  sort of thing. Why not set up
  a D.I.C. with her to chat                         DELETE
  about it in real time?
  She'll only be available to                       SAVE
  talk at five o'clock our time.
  Could you be around to chat                       PRINT
  with her then? Hope so!
  Rob, Josh and Tamsyn.
```

'Wincy,' Lauren muttered under her breath. 'Good, that means they've figured it out.' She turned and opened her mouth to yell to Allie. Then she thought better of it. She turned back to the e-mail.

She could see what her friends were trying to suggest. That she should attempt to get into a 'real time' conversation with Lester Pig over the Internet. DIC – Direct Internet Communication – was the equivalent on screen of a phone call. She guessed that they had a good reason for mentioning a specific time. Five o'clock. That was noon in Toronto.

Allie was all for Lauren doing her bit to help the guys over in England with their Black Widow problem. After all, she'd come up with the idea of seeding the message to them in that old typing exercise from way back when Allie had been trained as a secretary.

The exercise was used to help typists learn where all the keys were on a typewriter: it used every letter of the alphabet. Allie had no explanation for why it was half in English and half in German. She simply told Lauren, with a chuckle, that the sentence translated as: 'A pox on your children, old bean-bag, you've squashed my favourite pince-nez spectacles.'

But as eager as Allie was to see Black Widow squished, no way – not in a million years – would she go so far as to allow Lauren to miss school in order to try and engage Lester Pig in conversation. Allie had always insisted that, no matter what was going on over the Net, school came first.

In other words, Lauren was going to have to come up with a pretty good reason for being home at noon. A sure-fire, one-hundred-percent Allie-proof reason.

PRIMEWORKS Head Office, Portsmouth. 4.50 p.m.
Tamsyn and Josh got off the bus and took a final look at the street map. The street with the PRIME-WORKS head office was ringed in red. Only two minutes away.

'You do realize, don't you, that Rob's entire plan relies on Lauren managing to get a chat-line link with Karen at exactly the right time?' Josh said, not for the first time.

'Lauren will manage it,' Tamsyn said. 'Don't panic. Come on. We haven't got all day to stand around nattering.'

The office building was in a narrow side-street in a largely commercial area. The frontage was all steel and glass. Very modern. And very high-tech.

'Shouldn't we synchronize watches or something?' Josh asked as he stared in through the full-length tinted glass double doors.

'Don't be daft,' Tamsyn said. She pushed into the building with Josh close at her heels. It was time to set up part two of their plan to trap Karen Williams.

Tamsyn marched straight up to reception. 'Hi,

there,' she said to the man behind the tall counter. 'We're the students from Abbey School,' she smiled. 'You're expecting us. We're here to sort out some work experience. It's all been arranged. Mr Gibbons was expecting us half an hour ago. Would it be OK if we went straight up?'

The receptionist flipped through a sheaf of papers. 'I don't have any record of this,' he said. 'Who'd you say you were?'

'I'm Antonia Braithwaite,' Tamsyn said without batting an eyelid. 'And he's Edward, er, Trunk.'

The receptionist shook his head. 'I'll have to call up and let them know you're here.'

'Oh, please don't do that,' Tamsyn begged. 'It's going to look really bad if Mr Gibbons knows we've arrived late. Couldn't we just creep up there sort of unannounced? Then we can pretend we've been here for a while looking around.' Mr Gibbons was the man who ran the department in which Karen Williams worked. They'd found his name on the PRIMEWORKS site on the Net.

Tamsyn blazed a big, innocent, ingratiating smile at the man. He grinned back. 'Go on, then,' he said. 'Mr Gibbons' offices are on the third floor. Out of the lift and turn left, OK? You'll need a pass, though.' He gave them a pass each.

'Thanks,' Tamsyn said as she and Josh headed for the lifts. The doors opened almost immediately and they stepped inside.

Josh looked at her. 'Edward Trunk?' he said.

'Are you completely barmy? That's the name of the elephant in the Rupert cartoons!'

'It was all I could think of at short notice,' Tamsyn said. 'Nick gets Rupert Annuals for Christmas and I sometimes have a quick look through them. Anyway, that bloke obviously didn't make the connection, so what's the problem?'

'Oh, nothing,' Josh sighed as the lift slid smoothly upward towards the third floor. 'I suppose I should be grateful that you didn't tell him I was Kermit the Frog.'

Tamsyn laughed. 'I can see the resemblance,' she said. The lift purred to a halt and the doors glided open.

'OK,' Josh said as they stepped out into a long, brightly lit corridor. 'This is where things start to get serious.'

'Yeah, and remember what Rob said,' whispered Tamsyn in a low voice. 'Karen mustn't see us. At least, not before we get the chance to check out what's up on her screen.'

'Sheesh,' Josh hissed between his teeth. 'I hope Lauren gets her act together. We're wasting our time otherwise.'

'Look, just have a little faith, can't you?' Tamsyn said. 'You saw that e-mail from Lauren saying she'd be able to talk with Wincy at the right time. That means she's sorted something out, OK?' She walked soft-footedly along the corridor to the left. At the end were a pair of glass-panelled doors which led to a huge, open-plan office area.

The friends stared through the closed doors. Two dozen or more workstations were divided by chest-high screens. The office looked very busy, with people tapping away at their keyboards or marching briskly around with documents in their fists.

'Now what?' Josh whispered.

'We creep in there totally inconspicuously,' Tamsyn said quietly. 'We mustn't draw attention to ourselves. And keep your eyes peeled for Karen Williams. If anyone asks us what we're doing, just say—'

'Hello! What's all this?' boomed a voice that nearly made them jump out of their skins. They snapped their heads around. A short, plump man with a gleaming bald head had popped out of a side door and was staring at them with piercing blue eyes.

'What are you two up to, eh, eh?' His brows knitted as he barrelled up to them. 'You look very suspicious,' he said. 'Are you industrial spies sent by our rivals, eh?'

'No, of course not,' Josh said in surprise. 'We're … er …'

'Yes?' said the man. 'What exactly are you?'

'I can explain,' Tamsyn said, without the faintest idea of what to say next. 'Honest, I can explain.'

Toronto. 11.50 a.m. (UK time 4.50 p.m.)
Lauren lay in bed, doing her best to look as

pathetic and ill as possible. Allie sat on the edge of the bed, testing her granddaughter's forehead with her hand.

'You don't have a temperature,' her gran said. 'Is your stomach still hurting, honey?'

Lauren nodded weakly.

'I guess it must be something you ate,' her gran said.

Lauren had put on an Oscar-winning performance earlier that morning. Not too over-the-top, but not too wishy-washy, either. She'd judged it perfectly, letting Allie discover her curled over clutching her stomach and moaning softly to herself. Within two minutes Lauren had been packed off to bed. No school for you today, young lady!

Lauren didn't like deceiving her gran like that, but Rob and the others were relying on her. And Lauren had already decided that she'd confess all as soon as the job was done. She'd make up for it by being extra-special-wonderful to Allie for the whole of the next week.

Lauren just wished she'd managed to eat breakfast before being taken ill. She was ravenous.

'I think maybe I could try to eat something, Allie,' Lauren groaned above the rumblings of her complaining stomach.

'If you're sure,' her gran said. 'Is there anything in particular that you think you'd enjoy?'

'Soup, maybe?' Lauren tried a weak smile. 'I think I could manage a little chicken soup, or something like that.'

'I don't think we have any,' her gran said. She patted Lauren's hand. 'Now, how about I pop down to the store and see what I can find? Do you think you'll be OK on your own for half an hour or so?'

'I'm sure I will, Allie,' Lauren said bravely. That was exactly what she'd hoped her gran would say.

Her gran stood up. 'OK, then,' she said with a sympathetic smile. 'You just try to rest and I'll be back soon.'

Lauren sighed with a feeble grin. 'Thanks, Allie.'

Lauren waited until she heard the door to their apartment close.

'I'm really, really sorry, Allie,' she said as she flung the covers back and bounded out of bed. 'But I know you. You'd never have let me take time off school for this.' Lauren slid into her dressing gown and headed for the computer in the corner of their lounge.

'I just hope it's going to be worth it, that's all I can say,' she muttered as she booted up her computer and prepared to establish a Direct Internet Communication link with Lester Pig. Rob and Tamsyn and Josh must have chosen this particular time for a reason.

Lauren clicked on the menu item UTILITIES. The drop-down menu appeared and she clicked TALK. A dialogue-box appeared.

TALK TO WHICH USER ID?

Lauren tapped in:

LESTERPIG@PWORKS.CO.UK

There was a long pause.

Would Lester Pig bite? Lauren glanced at the time display at the top of her screen.

It was just coming up to twelve o'clock.

Well, she'd done everything she could. It all depended now on whether Lester Pig would take the bait.

CHAPTER 10

PRIMEWORKS Head Office. 5.00 p.m.

The tubby man's eyes bored into Tamsyn and Josh.

'Well?' he said testily. 'I'm waiting.'

'We're looking for Mr Gibbons,' Josh said.

'You've found him,' said the man.

Rats! Josh thought. Just my luck.

The man gestured towards himself. 'I'm Frank Gibbons. What do you want?'

'We've come from Abbey School,' Tamsyn said, her brain racing along at two hundred kilometres per hour. 'I'm Tamsyn Smith and this is Josh Allan. We ... we wondered if you found anything on that diskette Mr Findlay sent.'

Josh gave her an admiring look. Brilliant!

'Who's Mr Findlay?'

'He's our Head of Design and Technology,' Tamsyn gabbled. 'He sent you a diskette that we thought had a virus on it.'

'Oh, right!' The circular man nodded. 'Yes, I remember. Your school called us out a couple of days ago.' He shook his head. 'If we've received a disk from him, I certainly haven't seen it. Not that I necessarily would. It'd go straight to Karen. She's your front-line liaison officer. Karen Williams.' For the first time the man gave the ghost of a smile.

'I'll take you to her,' he said. 'Sorry I was a bit short with you. I've had one of those days. The switchboard is playing up.' He blinked at them. 'Modern technology, eh? We can communicate instantly with people on the other side of the world, but right now I can't even phone my own wife to tell her I'll be home late.' He shook his head. 'Astonishing!'

'You needn't bother taking us to Karen,' Tamsyn said quickly. 'You must be very busy. We'll find her OK.'

Mr Gibbons nodded and pointed through the glass doors. 'Her workstation is alongside the window on the left. At the far end behind those big cabinets. She'll be able to tell you anything you need to know.'

'Thanks.' Josh pushed the door open and the two of them walked into the long, open-plan office. He glanced around. Mr Gibbons was rolling importantly back down the corridor.

'Phew!' breathed Tamsyn. 'Close!'

'I think we should make like sour milk,' Josh said.

'Do what?'

'Separate,' Josh said with a grin.

'Oh, please!'

'Look, if we split up and come at her from

different directions, then if she spots one of us, it'll still give the other one time to check out her screen, right?'

'I suppose so. OK. I'll go that-a-way.' She made a hooked gesture to the right, indicating a route along the far wall. Good luck. And don't be conspicuous.'

'What – me?'

Tamsyn looked at him in that ill-fitting maroon sweatshirt that he'd grown too big for about a year ago. Josh was the sort of boy people noticed. Still, it couldn't be helped.

'The important thing,' she said as a final parting shot, 'is to look as if you know what you're doing, right?'

'Got it!'

They split up. Hardly anyone even glanced up as Josh walked along the rows of small workstations.

Just like battery chickens, he thought. He imagined Mr Gibbons throwing them a handful of millet every now and then. Come on, Josh. Pull yourself together. This is no time for daydreaming.

Tamsyn marched purposefully along on the far side from Josh. She took a quick look at her watch. It was five past five. As she walked the length of the room, Karen Williams' workstation gradually came into view from behind the barrier of the tall grey cabinets. The woman was at her desk with her back to Tamsyn, hunched over as though busy at her keyboard. From that distance it was impossible for Tamsyn to see what was up on her screen. But the large woman was definitely doing something that involved looking up at the screen and then typing.

Lauren must have made the Direct Internet Communication link. Now they would catch so-called Black Widow red-handed! And she thought she was so clever!

Toronto. 12.04 p.m. (UK time 5.04 p.m.)

Lauren nibbled at her fingernails. It had only been a minute or two since she had sent the TALK request to Lester Pig, but the time seemed to be dragging on forever with no response.

Then, suddenly her screen changed.

```
TALK> REQUEST ACCEPTED BY
LESTERPIG@PWORKS.CO.UK
```

Lauren began to type.

```
LAUREN> Hi! I just had to call and
congratulate you on that last checkmate.
I thought I played good, but you seem to
be able to catch me out every time.
```

She pressed the SEND button. Seconds later Lester Pig's reply appeared.

```
LESTERPIG> Thanks for the vote of
confidence, Lauren.
```

That was it. This wasn't going to be easy.

```
LAUREN> How did you learn to play chess so
well, LESTER? Hey, I can't keep calling
you by your User code. What's your name?

LESTERPIG> A few years ago I had a lot of
spare time, thanks to someone meddling in my
life. I learned a lot of things in that time.
```

Lester Pig hadn't responded to Lauren's question about her name.

```
LAUREN> That sounds interesting. What
happened?

LESTERPIG> I don't want to talk about
that.

LAUREN> Sorry. I guess I'm just naturally
nosy.

LESTERPIG> You know what curiosity did to
the cat, Lauren.

LAUREN> I beg your pardon? I don't
understand what you mean.

LESTERPIG> I think you do. Why do you want
to know my name?

LAUREN> I was just trying to be friendly.
```

There was a long pause. Lauren began to wonder whether Lester Pig was going to break the link.

```
LESTERPIG> I don't like people knowing
my name, Lauren. If people don't know who
you are, they can't interfere in your
life. Anonymous is safe. Solitude is
security.

LAUREN> That sounds like a pretty
miserable way of living. I think I'd
prefer to risk my life being interfered
with than be all on my own like that.

LESTERPIG> YOU KNOW NOTHING, YOU STUPID
LITTLE CHILD!
```

Lauren was knocked back in her seat by the
venom in Lester Pig's sudden flash. But it told
her something about Lester Pig that she hadn't
known until then. Lester Pig had called her a
child. Lauren was always at pains to keep her age
secret. So, how did Lester Pig know she was
young?

There was only one way Lester Pig could
know, and that was if she knew Lauren was a
friend of Rob and Tamsyn and the others.

Lauren licked her dry lips. She had no doubts
about it now: Lester Pig and Black Widow were
one and the same person!

PRIMEWORKS Head Office. 5.10 p.m.

Josh was now only a few metres away from
Karen's workstation. He could see her bent-over
back around the edge of the outmost cabinet. Her

screen was alive, but her head was blocking most of it. He thrust his hands into his pockets, trying to appear relaxed and at ease as he edged up to the cabinets.

Someone walked past, giving him a brief, uninterested glance. It looked like the PRIMEWORKS employees had enough to do without wondering why an unkempt schoolboy should be hanging around their office.

He slid half a step forwards and craned his neck to try and see over Karen Williams' shoulder. He was still too far away to be able to read what was on the screen, but it certainly did look to him like a Direct Internet Communication link. If he could just get a tiny bit closer without Karen noticing him.

Tamsyn had made her way right along to the far end of the office and was now in Karen's line of view. If Karen chose to look away from her screen and over to the right, she'd spot Tamsyn in an instant. Fortunately Karen seemed intent on her work.

Tamsyn felt eyes on her. She glanced around and saw a familiar face over the back of a computer. It was the quiet young woman who had helped Karen fix the virus. She was sitting at the PC, her hands poised over the keyboard, staring straight at Tamsyn with a most peculiar glint in her eyes.

For a split second Tamsyn felt quite creeped-out, but then the pale young woman broke eye contact and started to type.

A moment later there was a commotion from the far side of the room. Tamsyn glanced up.

Oh, no! Josh had fallen or tripped or something – either way, he was picking himself up off the floor and Karen Williams was standing over him with a ferocious expression on her face.

Josh had blown it! Without considering the consequences, Tamsyn ran to her friend's aid.

Abbey School. 5.10 p.m.

Rob was still in the Computer Club room, waiting for news from his friends. He hadn't called his mother yet for his regular lift home. And he was fretting about how Tamsyn and Josh were getting on.

He looked at his watch. There wasn't much time left. The plan was that one or the other of them would ring the school as soon as they found out anything over at PRIMEWORKS. There were still plenty of people around to answer the phones at Abbey School. Josh or Tamsyn would ask for Mr Findlay. They knew he would be there – he was taking an adult night-school class that evening.

Either the call would be to tell him that Karen Williams was responsible for the virus, or, at worst, to tell him that another virus was in the system, due to trigger at six o'clock that evening and cause a huge amount of damage, and to warn him to close everything down. He'd have some explaining to do if he did that!

To fill in the waiting time, Rob was going through the Abbey web site files again, hoping that something might pop up that would explain why Karen – if it was Karen – had such a downer on the school. One thing was absolutely certain: Black Widow had a reason for the mayhem she was about to unleash. But what?

Mr Findlay came into the room.

'Oh, hello, Rob. Still here?' he said. 'I had a slip of paper with the names of this evening's students on it. Have you seen it? Ah – is that it?'

He scooped up a piece of paper from in front of Rob with their workings-out of Lauren's e-mail on it. It was the piece of paper which also had their previous jottings on it. Rob had been looking at it while he waited.

He frowned. 'Barbara Wilde?' he said, reading it. 'That rings a bell.'

Rob looked sharply at him.

'Good heavens,' Mr Findlay said. 'I know now! That young woman from PRIMEWORKS! I thought I recognized her. Barbara Wilde! Of course! She was a student here a few years ago. I had a bit of a run-in with her.'

That was it! That was the link!

'You mean Barbara Wilde is calling herself Karen Williams now?' Rob gasped.

'Hmm? Oh, no, no, no. Not her. The other one. I refused to allow her to sit an exam because she hadn't put enough effort into her work. She ended up sitting the exam in October. The last time I saw her was when she gave me a stream of abuse for interfering in her life!'

Mr Findlay put the paper down and walked out of the room before Rob had a chance to recover from this amazing revelation. 'I'm astounded that anyone thought she was stable enough to employ!' Mr Findlay said in parting. 'I always thought there was something very strange about her.'

Mr Findlay disappeared down the corridor.

Rob sat there with his mouth hanging open in shock. It was the other one. Not Karen at all! Josh and Tamsyn were stalking the wrong person!

CHAPTER 11

Toronto. 12.11 p.m. (UK time 5.11 p.m.)

```
LAUREN> Hey, don't get mad at me.
What have I ever done to you? I
just want us to be friends.

LESTERPIG> I don't think so, Lauren.
I don't make friends. I'm going
now.

LAUREN> No, wait. Forget all the
personal stuff, *OK*? Just talk
to me about chess.
```

Lauren bit her lip as she waited for the reply.
LESTERPIG hadn't broken the link, but she
wasn't sending anything either.

```
LAUREN> Are you still there?

LESTERPIG> I've just seen your
friend Tamsyn. Nice try, Lauren.
I won't treat you people so well next
time. Goodbye.
```

Josh had leaned just that little bit too far in his efforts to see over Karen Williams' shoulder. He lost balance, grabbed at the nearest thing to stop himself falling, and found himself sprawled on the floor with a heap of file-folders scattered around him.

Karen jumped clear out of her chair at the sudden crash directly behind her.

'What the heck …!' She stared at Josh as if she couldn't quite believe her eyes.

Josh scrambled to his feet. 'I slipped,' he said. Faces from all over the office were turned towards the centre of activity.

'What are you doing here?' Karen asked.

'Er … nothing. Just … um … getting up.'

'*What?*'

Tamsyn came running up. 'We've got you!' she yelled at Karen. 'We know what you've been up to – Black Widow!'

Karen goggled at her. 'Are you totally potty?'

Josh thrust out his arm, pointing to the screen. 'It's no use pretending!' he shouted. 'The evidence is right there!'

They all looked round at the screen.

```
BELINDA> Thanks for the Chocolate and
Walnut Syrup Tart recipe. You forgot to
say how much golden syrup to add.

KAREN> 120ml (8tbsp) should do the trick.
```

```
BELINDA> Great. How long do I cook it for?

KAREN> Gas mark 4. 20 to 30 minu
```

'Oh!' Josh's eyes nearly popped right out of his head and bounced off the screen. 'Oh – cripes!'

Karen stared at the two of them, her fists on her broad hips. 'So? What are you pair – the diet police, or something? Can't a person swap recipes any more?'

'No, er, yes,' Tamsyn gasped. 'We thought you were … we … you … um … I think maybe we've made a mistake.' She edged towards Josh. 'I think it's probably best if we go now.'

Tamsyn linked arms with Josh and the two of them backed away from the astounded Karen.

'She wasn't talking to Lauren,' Josh whispered out of the corner of his mouth.

'I know. I saw.'

'What do we do now?'

'Stop right there!' Karen said, advancing on them. 'I don't know what you pair of loonies are up to, but I think Mr Gibbons will want to see you before you disappear.'

Karen marched the two friends the length of the office and out into the corridor. She stopped and hammered on the same side door from which Mr Gibbons had emerged earlier.

There was no reply. Karen opened the door. The office was empty.

'OK,' Karen said. 'I'm going to find the boss.' She waved a warning finger at them. 'If either of you move one step from here, I'll come back and I'll sit on your heads. Get the picture?'

They nodded. Karen's picture was all too vivid!

Karen went storming down the corridor in search of Mr Gibbons. Josh and Tamsyn looked at each other.

They didn't move.

PRIMEWORKS Head Office. 5.20 p.m.

'Hey! You two!' They recognized the voice that came booming along the corridor. It was Mr Gibbons, and he sounded somewhat ticked off. 'I want you!'

Beam me up, Scotty, Josh thought as they turned to face Mr Gibbons. He stormed up to them like a runaway train, waving a sheet of paper at them.

'What's the idea of telling your friends you can be contacted here!' he stormed. 'This is an office, not a chatline. I will not have my equipment clogged up with this sort of thing.' He brandished the sheet of paper under Josh's nose.

It didn't sound as though the cause of his annoyance was anything to do with Karen Williams. Mr Gibbons was angry with them for an entirely different reason.

'What is it?' Tamsyn asked, her head wobbling around as she tried to focus on the writing on the page.

'An e-mail from someone called Rob Zanelli,' Mr Gibbons declared. 'And if you—'

'Excuse me,' Tamsyn said, snatching the paper out of his hand. 'Can I see that?'

```
Tamsyn Smith and Josh Allan
No time to explain. It isn't Karen. It's
the *other* one!
Rob Zanelli.
```

'The other one,' Tamsyn gasped. She spun on her heel and ran for the glass doors. She crashed through with Josh and Mr Gibbons right behind her. Mr Gibbons was going pink with indignation.

Tamsyn stared towards the workstation where she had seen the pale young woman with the peculiar eyes.

The workstation was deserted. Tamsyn tore across the room with Mr Gibbons and Josh in pursuit.

'Where has she gone?' Tamsyn shouted, banging her hands down on the back of the pale woman's empty seat. She stared at Mr Gibbons. 'What's the name of the person who works here?'

'Barbara Wilde, but I think you'd better explain …'

Josh spun around, hoping to catch some glimpse of Barbara Wilde.

'She was here a few minutes ago!' Tamsyn shouted. She stared at the computer screen.

LAUREN> Are you still there?

LESTERPIG> I've just seen your friend
Tamsyn. Nice try, Lauren. I won't treat
you people so well next time. Goodbye.

'It was her!' Tamsyn almost screamed.

'Will someone please explain what these insane children are doing here!' Mr Gibbons shouted.

Josh sucked in a deep, deep breath. Every eye in the room was on them. This was going to have to be a very good explanation indeed.

Abbey School. 5.50 p.m.

Rob stared at his watch and then stared at the closed door of the room in which Mr Findlay was about to start his evening Tech. Class. Only ten minutes to go!

It was over half an hour since he'd tried to phone PRIMEWORKS, only to keep getting the engaged signal. Rob wasn't to know their switchboard was faulty and they couldn't receive or make telephone calls. But what he did know was that Josh and Tamsyn needed this new information about Black Widow right away.

Mr Findlay had vanished. Rob had to act alone. And the only thing Rob could think of was to send an e-mail to Tamsyn and Josh actually at PRIME-WORKS Head Office and hope for the best.

And then Rob waited. He didn't want to warn Mr Findlay too soon in case he shut down the system straight away and somehow alerted Black Widow – Barbara Wilde – to the fact that they were on to her. She mustn't be given the opportunity to cover her tracks.

But if nothing happened in the next five minutes, Rob had decided he'd just have to interrupt Mr Findlay's class and try to convince him to shut Abbey's complete system down before the Big Bang hit!

Rob was out in the corridor feeling very edgy. Where on earth were Tamsyn and Josh? Had they even received his e-mail? A door burst open behind him and he spun around to look.

'You took your time!' Rob yelled as Tamsyn and Josh came hurtling into the Technical Block.

They had driven over there in Karen's car. Tamsyn and Josh had raced on ahead while Karen parked, shouting back instructions to her on how to get to the Technical Block.

'We got here as quick as we could!' panted Tamsyn. 'Karen is right behind us.'

Rob opened the classroom door. 'Do you know how to stop the virus?'

'No,' gasped Josh.

Rob snapped a glance at the wall clock. It was two minutes to six.

'Rob Zanelli,' Mr Findlay said in an irritated voice, 'how many times have I told you people not to disturb me while I'm teaching?'

'Sorry,' said Tamsyn. 'There's no time to explain.'

She burst into the room-full of startled adults. '
need to do this now!' She dived across the room
and all but rammed Mr Findlay off his seat.

'What on earth is going on?' he gasped
staring in disbelief as Rob and Josh came up
to Tamsyn.

'Quick!' Josh groaned. The clock showed one
minute to six.

'I thought you said you couldn't stop the
virus?' Rob said.

'We can't,' Tamsyn panted, her fingers flying
over the keyboard. 'But Karen told us how we
can slow it down!'

'Tamsyn! Stop that right now and explain
yourself!' Mr Findlay demanded.

'Just one second,' Tamsyn said. 'There's an
other virus in the system!'

'But, how do you know—'

Tamsyn lifted a hand. 'Done it!' she said with a
sigh of relief. She slumped back in the chair.

'Done what?' asked Rob.

Josh pointed at the screen.

At that moment the hands on the wall clock hi
six o'clock.

Nothing happened.

Rob looked at the computer screen. The system
clock read 17.00. Five o'clock.

'You put the time back,' Rob said with a grin
'That's brilliant.'

Josh saw the baffled expression on M
Findlay's face. 'The virus was set to go off at si:
o'clock this evening,' he explained. 'Karen told u

that we could slow it down by putting the system clock back an hour!'

'Did you get there in time?' called Karen as she came puffing into the classroom.

'Sure did!' said Tamsyn.

'Excellent,' said Karen with a big smile. 'And now let's find that little bomb of yours and put it out of action.'

Tamsyn gave up her seat and Karen got to work at the computer.

Mr Findlay made a few wordless noises that sounded like a balloon deflating.

Karen's fingers danced over the keys and the screen changed and changed like a kaleidoscope as she searched. 'Ha!' She jammed her thumb down on a key. 'Gotcha!'

'I don't understand what's going on here,' Mr Findlay said.

'We can explain,' Tamsyn said, giving him a reassuring smile.

'Have you disabled it?' Rob asked.

Karen nodded, her eyes glued to the screen. 'I'm pretty sure I have,' she said. 'Unless Babs slipped something new in. One way to check. And that's by putting the time right.'

All eyes were on the clock display as Karen altered it to read 18.02.

Karen looked around at their anxious expressions, then laughed. 'Anyone got a spare bar of chocolate or something?' she said. 'All this rushing about killing viruses makes me hungry!'

She used the mouse to clear the screen, then she typed:

```
No applause, please, just throw money!
```

Mr Findlay stared at his three grinning students.

'And now,' he said slowly, 'will someone kindly explain to me exactly what is going on here?'

Abbey School. Friday 18th October, 7.40 a.m.

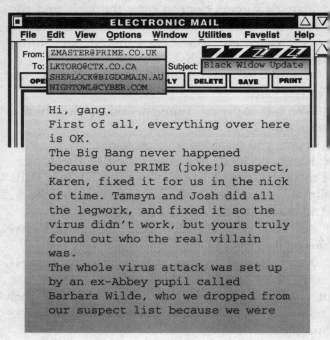

```
┌──────────────────────────────────────────┐
│ ■      ELECTRONIC MAIL              △ ▽    │
├──────────────────────────────────────────┤
│ File  Edit  View  Options  Window  Utilities  Favelist  Help │
├──────────────────────────────────────────┤
│ From: ZMASTER@PRIME.CO.UK        ⁊⁊⁊⁊⁊⁊    │
│ To: LKTORO@CTX.CO.CA      Subject: Black Widow Update │
│      SHERLOCK@BIGDOMAIN.AU                 │
│ OPE  NIGHTOWL@CYBER.COM    LY  DELETE  SAVE  PRINT │
├──────────────────────────────────────────┤
│   Hi, gang.                                │
│   First of all, everything over here       │
│   is OK.                                    │
│   The Big Bang never happened              │
│   because our PRIME (joke!) suspect,       │
│   Karen, fixed it for us in the nick       │
│   of time. Tamsyn and Josh did all         │
│   the legwork, and fixed it so the         │
│   virus didn't work, but yours truly       │
│   found out who the real villain           │
│   was.                                      │
│   The whole virus attack was set up        │
│   by an ex-Abbey pupil called              │
│   Barbara Wilde, who we dropped from       │
│   our suspect list because we were         │
└──────────────────────────────────────────┘
```

INTERNET DETECTIVES

```
told her family had emigrated. Well,
maybe they did - but *she* certainly
didn't!
```

'Tell them why she had it in for the school,'
Tamsyn said, leaning across Rob's shoulder as he
typed.

'I will if you give me a chance,' Rob said.

'And don't forget to give Lauren three cheers
for all her help,' Josh added.

Rob rolled his eyes heavenwards. 'I was just
going to,' he said.

'Well, go on then,' Tamsyn said, jogging Rob's
arm. 'We haven't got all day, you know.'

```
This *Black Widow* was a bit of an
obsessive nut!
She was attacking the school to
get our Mr Findlay. That's why the
first virus was triggered by the
date of his birthday.
Apparently, five years back, he
refused to let her sit her A-Level
exam because her attendance at
school had been so poor that he
thought she needed more time to
catch up. But Wilde had been
promised a place at University
*that* summer, so long as she
passed her exams.
According to Mr Findlay, she was
```

very angry that she wasn't allowed
to sit the D & T exam until the
resits in October, because that
meant she had to wait a whole
extra year before she could get
into University. So, you see, she
directly blamed him for wasting an
entire year of her life.
By the way, folks, I ought to
point out that Wilde isn't exactly
normal. In fact, she's as nutty
as a chestnut tree in Autumn!

'You can say that again,' said Tamsyn. 'You'd
better fill them in on the bad news, as well.'

There's good news and there's bad
news. First of all, a big round of
applause to Lauren, without whom
etcetera... Hey, Allie! Don't be
too hard on her, please, she was
brilliant.
The good news is that we managed
to stop Black Widow's nasty
scheme. The bad news is that the
police haven't found her yet.
Latest info is that she's vanished
from the room she rents. But all
her computer equipment has been
confiscated too, so, basically,
she's had it!
Rob, Tamsyn & Josh -
Spiderbusters!

Mail:

Rob looked round at his friends.

'Will that do?' he asked.

'Put a PS,' Josh suggested. 'Something like: that'll teach her to tangle with us! She won't do that again in a hurry.'

Rob was about to start typing when Tamsyn grabbed his wrist.

'No,' she said. 'Don't put that. It's tempting fate.'

'Do what?' Josh asked.

Tamsyn looked at them. 'She's still out there,' she said solemnly. 'And she hates us.'

'Don't worry about it,' Rob said. 'She wouldn't dare show her face around here again.'

'I hope you're right,' Tamsyn said. 'I've just got a bad feeling that we haven't heard the last of the Black Widow.'

michael coleman

ACCESS DENIED

'TOP SECRET. MILITARY ACCESS ONLY.'

'That's it then,' said Josh, looking at the flashing screen. 'We can't search any further!'
   'Oh yes you can,' said his friend. 'If you know how.'

The Internet Detectives are trying to identify the mysterious creature they discovered hidden on a museum warship. But it seems that sinister powers are determined to stop them. As Josh, Tom and their friends around the world push their investigations to the limit, they find that the Net can be a very dangerous place indeed ...

Other books in the series ▷

michael coleman

NET BANDITS

TAMSYN, GET HELP
:-((¬:-D :-U i-)

A new message suddenly appears on
Tamsyn's computer screen from the
mystery kid who calls himself
ZMASTER. Is it a joke, or is he in real
trouble? Tamsyn and Josh are sure
something is seriously wrong.
But how can they help him when they
don't know who he is?
Electronic messages flash round the
globe as friends thousands of miles
apart try to find a boy in terrible
danger . . .

But will the Internet reveal its secrets
in time?

Other books in the series ▶

michael coleman

ESCAPE KEY

The man's face stared out at them from the computer screen.
  'It is him!' exclaimed Rob.

The photograph, flashed instantly from Australia via the Internet, sets Rob, Tamsyn and Josh on a thrilling hunt for a man wanted by the police on two continents. They've seen him once already, but they've no idea where he is now. With the help of brilliant detective work by their friends on the Net, they start to track down their mysterious suspect . . .

Other books in the series ▷

michael coleman

SPEED SURF

**Gis Igne's ypm Gxliqy.
H$'s sssli3g a zqcht c=@12d
#wMqo zmi 0jr.**

The message on the computer screen
is nonsense. But Josh, Rob and Tamsyn
are sure it contains a clue to the
identity of an international art thief.
The scrambled words have come over
the Internet from a single-handed
yachtsman in mid-Atlantic, just as his
computer power began to fail. Now
they must decipher his message and,
with time running out, set a trap for a
dangerous enemy . . .

Other books in the series ▷

michael coleman

CYBER FEUD

Tamsyn pointed at the screen. 'The system says you logged in yesterday.'
'But I didn't!' cried Josh. 'You've got to believe me!'

Years before, Josh Allen's father was blamed for a crime he didn't commit. Can Josh, Tamsyn and Rob use their contacts on the Net to prove Mr Allen's innocence after all these years?
The trail leads them round the world – but only to discover that somebody else is always one step ahead of them. Then Josh himself is accused of a crime. He swears he's innocent. Who is making history repeat itself? And why?

Other books in the series ▷